MY WIFE'S AFFAIR

MY WIFE'S AFFAIR

N A N C Y   W O O D R U F F

AMY EINHORN BOOKS

Published by G. P. Putnam's Sons

a member of Penguin Group (USA) Inc.

New York

AMY EINHORN BOOKS
Published by G. P. Putnam's Sons
Publishers Since 1838
Published by the Penguin Group
Penguin Group (USA) Inc., 375 Hudson Street, New York, New York 10014, USA •
Penguin Group (Canada), 90 Eglinton Avenue East, Suite 700, Toronto, Ontario M4P 2Y3, Canada
(a division of Pearson Penguin Canada Inc.) • Penguin Books Ltd, 80 Strand,
London WC2R 0RL, England • Penguin Ireland, 25 St Stephen's Green, Dublin 2, Ireland
(a division of Penguin Books Ltd) • Penguin Group (Australia), 250 Camberwell Road, Camberwell,
Victoria 3124, Australia (a division of Pearson Australia Group Pty Ltd) •
Penguin Books India Pvt Ltd, 11 Community Centre, Panchsheel Park, New Delhi–110 017, India •
Penguin Group (NZ), 67 Apollo Drive, Rosedale, North Shore 0632, New Zealand
(a division of Pearson New Zealand Ltd) • Penguin Books (South Africa) (Pty) Ltd,
24 Sturdee Avenue, Rosebank, Johannesburg 2196, South Africa

Penguin Books Ltd, Registered Offices: 80 Strand, London WC2R 0RL, England

Library of Congress Cataloging-in-Publication Data

Woodruff, Nancy.
My wife's affair / Nancy Woodruff.
p.   cm.
ISBN 978-0-399-15629-8
1. Married people—Fiction.   2. Americans—England—Fiction.   3. Actresses—Fiction.
4. Acting—Fiction.   5. Adultery—Fiction.   6. Jordan, Dorothy, 1761–1816—Fiction.
7. London (England)—Fiction.   I. Title.
PS3573.O62645M92   2010   2009036348
813'.54—dc22

Printed in the United States of America
1   3   5   7   9   10   8   6   4   2

Book design by Meighan Cavanaugh

This is a work of fiction. Names, characters, places, and incidents either are the product
of the author's imagination or are used fictitiously, and any resemblance to actual persons,
living or dead, businesses, companies, events, or locales is entirely coincidental.

While the author has made every effort to provide accurate telephone numbers and
Internet addresses at the time of publication, neither the publisher nor the author assumes
any responsibility for errors, or for changes that occur after publication. Further,
the publisher does not have any control over and does not assume any
responsibility for author or third-party websites or their content.

APR 4 2010

For Mark,

with love

Author's Note

Dora Jordan (1761–1816) was the preeminent comic actress of her time. It is hard to overstate how famous she was for her portrayal of Rosalind in *As You Like It*, a role she played from the age of twenty-six to the age of fifty-three. I first encountered Mrs. Jordan's portrait at Apsley House in London and subsequently came to admire her via Claire Tomalin's brilliant biography *Mrs Jordan's Profession: The Story of a Great Actress and a Future King*. The exhaustive bibliography in Ms. Tomalin's book led me in turn to additional historical works about Mrs. Jordan, none so compelling as Ms. Tomalin's. I took small liberties with time and sequencing when writing *Shakespeare's Woman*, the play within the novel, but I aimed to remain faithful to both the facts of Mrs. Jordan's life—insofar as they are known—and the warmth of her voice. In writing the play, I drew heavily upon Mrs. Jordan's letters as collected by Arthur Aspinall in *Mrs Jordan and Her Family, Being the Unpublished Letters of Mrs Jordan and the Duke of Clarence, Later William IV*. Likewise invaluable was the spectacularly named, anonymously penned book *The Great*

Illegitimates: Public and Private Life of That Celebrated Actress, Miss Bland, Otherwise Mrs Ford, or Mrs Jordan; Late Mistress of HRH the Duke of Clarence, Now King William IV, Founder of the Fitzclarence Family . . . *accompanied by numerous remarks and anecdotes of illustrious and fashionable characters*. Also tremendously illuminating was *The Life of Mrs Jordan*, by Mrs. Jordan's contemporary James Boaden.

For an understanding of tithe barns I am most indebted to James W. Griswold's *A Guide to Medieval English Tithe Barns*, as well as to my family for enduring numerous forays into the English countryside.

ACKNOWLEDGMENTS

In London, Sharon Bassin, Celeste Cole, Catherine Davidson, Alex George, and Cathy Hoey offered more enthusiasm and help than any writer deserves. The British Library provided hours and hours of shelter and space for writing and research. In the United States, Renee Bacher, Ann Darby, Sara Eckel, and Camilla Trinchieri provided unwavering encouragement. Henny Russell generously shared with me important details about the lives of actors. Paul Elie read the manuscript and offered his always spot-on criticism. Maria Massie and Amy Einhorn, agent and editor, respectively, are models of perfection. I thank them all.

MY WIFE'S AFFAIR

We try, we husbands and fathers, we really do. I just want to tell you that. We may not find the perfect triceratops pajamas on sale four months before the birthday; it wouldn't occur to us to set up a magic closet full of stickers and Silly Putty for them on days when they're sick or scared or we just love them so much. We don't always remember to ask about swimming lessons or the spelling test, and we've been known to come home late at night and go straight to bed without looking in on the kids (how this appalled Georgie).

I admit all of this, but also say that when we walk in the door at the end of the working day we don't ask for peace and quiet and the day's mail, but instead—so grateful that they're ours—just for those little bodies coming at us in a rush.

Not that Georgie was any angel of the house. If you passed her on the street, her orange scarf the only bit of color against a full black ensemble and all that wavy brown hair, you wouldn't necessarily picture her wrapping the dinosaur pajamas in dinosaur paper. But she did, just the way she knew when to give them *Curious George* and when they would love *Charlotte's Web*, while all I could feebly remember was that I had read *The Hobbit* sometime in junior high.

Because she had these passions, you see—that's how she knew what to do. She threw herself into motherhood the same way she had thrown herself into acting. Or into me. It was the only way she could possibly love what she loved, and she was spectacular at it—until she tried to balance her passions. Georgie knew, but would not quite believe, that passions do not survive the weighing of one against the other.

Georgie. I did call her Georgie-girl sometimes, though it wasn't as corny as it might have been if we were older and the song more than a catchy tune our fathers used to hum.

Even now I can imagine her walking in and my saying, "Hey, there, Georgie-girl," and the boys all over their mother, and me, I guess, like one of them.

I would do anything for her.

I would do anything for her.

Still.

I could begin, I suppose, when Georgie and I met. Manhattan: she was an actor/waiter, and I was a writer with a boring day job near her restaurant. Do I even need to say *struggling?* Or do I jump six years later, when she was four months pregnant with Fergus and we decided to get married? Or to nineteen months after that, when the twins were born and Georgie was left an exhausted mother in a fourth-floor walk-up, a Rapunzel with three boys under two who couldn't even leave the apartment by herself?

Perhaps the story begins in that house in New Jersey, the one we fled to when it became impossible to stay in the city any longer. It was a fair trade, Georgie said, one kind of prison for another. She could leave the house now, but with no sidewalks to walk on, no parks or coffee shops to stroll to, she could go nowhere without wedging three children into three car seats in the huge Volvo station wagon she was terrified to drive.

For a time Georgie lost herself there, to a life she felt was someone else's. She lost herself for almost four years to a place that cut her off from her version of the world. And then she found herself again, in England, and perhaps I should begin there—where the end began, unless you are the type who believes it was there all along, hovering, waiting to swoop from the start.

England. The tithe barn. I have left a third of my life there, fully half of my heart, and I can tell you honestly now that I would have abandoned everything to those walls if it hadn't been for those sons who needed me, the beautiful boys who went to England with two parents who loved them, and returned part of a family forever in ruins.

*I*t was a narrow street of seventeen pastel-colored houses. Ours was the tender pink of a seashell's interior. The house to the left was white, to the right, pale yellow, and up and down the street these colors repeated, with varying shades of duck's egg, mint, and lilac added to them. They were tiny attached cottages, looking as if they might well be inhabited by a badger with a frilly apron or a bonneted Mrs. Squirrel.

When Georgie and I house-hunted in London (we had only four days), every cobbled mews or garden square or terraced crescent we turned down was more beautiful than the last. But this—this was the most adorable street Georgie had ever seen, even more adorable than West Eleventh Street in Greenwich Village, which to her mind had previously held the prize. How could the English stand it, she wondered, how could they play out their daily lives on a set this picturesque?

It was a four-story house, but the scale was diminutive, the staircases both narrow and shallow, so that our big American feet had to bow out in order to fit on the steps. There were two small sitting rooms on the ground floor, a kitchen in the basement, a sunny square room for the boys upstairs, and a master suite at the very top of the house. The word *nursery* came to Georgie's mind when she saw the boys' room, though the boys were too old for a nursery. Fergus was five and a half years old when we moved to London, and Liam and Jack had just turned four—we'd held their birthday party in our suburban backyard the week before the movers came to begin packing up the house.

The London house came furnished—"from spoons to sofa," the estate agent said. This meant there were dishes and silverware in the kitchen cabinets, sheets and towels in the linen cupboard, prints on the wall, and little dried flower arrangements all around. All we had to do was unpack our suitcases. Georgie loved that. She hadn't wanted to bring our hodgepodge of furniture, all greatly unloved pieces we'd bought at tag sales and consignment shops in hurried desperation to fill the big empty rooms of that suburban house. She was happy to leave that, all of it, in a warehouse in New Jersey.

My assignment in London was for three years, an expatriate fairy tale replete with perks and stipends and income-equalization measures designed to make Georgie and me feel as if every financial woe we'd ever had was about to be lifted. I had put my hand up for the assignment as soon as I heard about it, seeing it as an adventure, but more than an adventure, as a way to extricate ourselves, if only temporarily, from a way of life I had gotten used to over time but Georgie had not.

The little house even came with a housekeeper, an elegant Spanish woman named Hortensia. *She's a real treasure,* our landlady said, *and she knows the house so well. She's been coming every Thursday afternoon for six years.* She implored us to take her, and we didn't refuse.

It was just like stepping into someone else's life, walking down their little street, opening their sweet front door, and taking it from there. Georgie was an actress; she was good at this, she was great at it—taking on a new role, never looking back, turning herself full force into someone else—especially after playing a part that had wearied her for so long.

The boys were to be in school all day. This came as a shock to everybody. In the States, Fergus would just be starting half-day kindergarten, and the twins would still be squishing Play-Doh and making pasta necklaces three mornings a week at preschool. But things began earlier in England: Fergus was already behind, we were told (still not reading at five and a half!), and Jack and Liam were to start in right away—reading and writing and doing their maths.

The relocation consultant found five private schools willing to take all three boys. Georgie had far more opinions on these things than I did. It had taken her months to find the right preschool in New Jersey, but there was no way she could apply that fervor to the two days we had to make our choice.

"I don't have nearly enough time to agonize over this," she complained, and in the end the decision was more a process of elimination. She didn't like the American School, which felt to her like a cross between a state penitentiary and the headquarters of a Fortune 500 company, and the two all-boys schools sent me into irrational speculation about circle jerks and *Lord of the Flies*. The fourth school had a headmaster so cold Georgie wanted to run from the room after five minutes in his presence. ("Could you even *see* him with a four-year-old on his lap?" she asked me, thinking of the twins' old nursery school teacher, with his ponytail and Birkenstocks, his endless bear hugs.)

We were left with a coed school in a beautiful white stucco Georgian building just across from Hyde Park. Because it was summer, we saw nothing but empty classrooms and bare bulletin boards, so we had to judge by the feel of the hallways and the headmaster's smile. He seemed like someone who would be on a child's side, Georgie thought, and as we stood at one of the huge classroom windows and watched the shiny black horses of the Queen's Household Cavalry canter across the royal park, she said, "This is a dream. *I* want to go to this school."

On the first day of school she took a picture of the boys in their school uniforms—red V-neck sweaters, gray flannel shorts, matching gray caps, and the red ties she was going to have to teach them all to tie. I do not need to look at that picture for my eyes to see the boys as they looked that day—three little soldiers in their red-and-gray uniforms, Fergus smiling shyly, Jack clowning, and tough-guy Liam turning his head, looking for the action like a small-town thug on a Saturday night. Georgie and I are dark, and Fergus took after us, with Georgie's curls, but the twins, in some recessive revolt, were blonder than blond, with honey-brown eyes and very fair skin. Fergus stood a number of inches taller than the twins, and despite his timidity he had a tall, almost stately bearing, while the twins were still outgrowing their toddler legs. They seemed barely more than babies to me, but Fergus, Fergus already seemed to have embarked on his life. Still, in those uniforms, the boys looked tremendously alike. Can I be forgiven for even once thinking of them as *the boys, my sons*, rather than as three astonishing individuals?

We had been in the country less than seventy-two hours and the boys were pale with jet lag, but Georgie didn't want them to miss the first day of school. She dragged them along the broad sidewalks, trying to keep them from hitting each other or losing their caps or falling into traffic. When you have three children and only two hands it is always the child you need to keep hold of who wants to run ahead.

She watched mothers, fathers, and nannies all around her walking their children to school. Girls in purple-striped dresses and boater hats. Tiny boys in heavy green blazers that seemed made for their fathers. Boys and girls both in what appeared to be Oliver Twist–style breeches and caps, mustard yellow in color and hideously ugly. A sweet group of girls looking like little Alices in gorgeous blue dresses with bric-a-brac trim. Unlike Liam, Jack, and Fergus, the English children seemed to know how to behave, gliding serenely schoolward in their uniforms while Georgie yelled at her little American boys, threatening them, yanking, clutching, and separating them.

"Mom, Liam smells," Jack said when they walked past a pungent dumpster in front of a building undergoing renovation.

"You idiot dumbhead," Liam said, lunging at Jack, and Georgie had to keep them physically apart while Fergus, who as a rule never stopped plying us with questions about life, kept up his constant commentary, oblivious to everything except when he demanded an answer: "I don't get life. I mean, does God just keep making people and more people and that's all he ever does? How does he do it? Some people are so tiny, like kids and babies, and he makes the grown-ups, too. How does he know what size to use? Dinosaurs are giants compared to people. Dinosaurs' brains are tiny. Not people's. I have a big brain. Do dinosaurs have the same brains as people? Mom? Mom?

Mom, I said, DO DINOSAURS HAVE THE SAME BRAINS AS PEOPLE?" He was whacking her with his cap by now and she yelled, "I don't know," while trying to keep Liam and Jack off of each other. She had no idea how anybody was going to get them to sit still long enough to teach them anything.

The twins' teacher, Miss Arabella, was sunny and blond and so small that Jack and Liam almost reached her shoulders. She had them enthralled immediately with her smile. Fergus's teacher was Miss Joanne—unsmiling, sterner. She shook hands with Fergus at the door and told him to find a desk and begin doing the work that was set out for him. Georgie had expected to stay for a while and settle the children—read them a story or do a puzzle with them while they grew more comfortable in their new classrooms—but Miss Joanne stood firmly in the doorway saying *hello children, goodbye parents.*

Georgie lingered in the school entranceway, already missing her sons, half waiting for at least one of them to come after her. When that didn't happen she began to walk slowly away from the school, her gait quickening as she stepped into the morning routines of the strangers on the street. Three boys; she had thought she would be making sandwiches for the rest of her life, yet there they were, at school (where a hot lunch was served; no sandwiches required), and here she was, in a beautiful ancient city, an entire day to herself for practically the first time in five years.

She passed a newsstand and bought a *Time Out*, then found a French café on Thackeray Street, where she ordered a coffee and sat on a check-cushioned bench at a table in the back. Two men sat next to her, talking rapidly in French. Everyone in the café was smoking. Carelessly refolded newspapers and copies of *Hello!* and *Paris Match* strewn around empty tables seemed to Georgie to contain the throbbing heart of the real world.

She felt suddenly light as air. Everything in her life had changed. Everything, it felt, had been restored. This wasn't her city, but it was a great city, possibly second best in her mind, a city that excited her, and a city that she knew. She had done a year at the University of London during college, and a couple of times in her twenties she had come to the UK, touring with small productions. Still, it was hard to believe that the nonstop motion of the past five years of child-raising, the demons of aging and dreams deferred, the rush and strain of the move, had now deposited her in such a splendid, quiet place, all on her own. *I could go to a museum,* she thought; *I could go to a matinee.*

Nevertheless, a half-hour later she called me from home, sobbing. "My boys," she said, "Peter, my boys are gone," all the while laughing at her own tears.

*M*e? In those days I was a journalist, a business journalist. If you like, you can read that as Failed Novelist.

At least you know my name now. Peter. Peter Martin, as bland and symmetrical a name as the American Midwest could produce circa 1964.

I had met Georgie more than a dozen years earlier, when I was writing my first novel. When I couldn't publish that one, I began a second, and when that one didn't sell either, I stopped—not writing, necessarily, but trying to be a writer. I sound cavalier now, but each of those two books took me more than four years to write, and before that there were years of unpublished short stories.

Even now I can hear Georgie say, "For God's sake, Peter, don't tell them *that*. Peter, Peter, Peter, the world is a girl you're trying to get to sleep with you, and you'll never succeed if you tell her your failures."

The savvy Manhattanite and the modest midwesterner—she had always had a lot to teach me.

When I was still in graduate school, I published a story in *The New Yorker*. They paid me ten thousand dollars. I thought I had it made, but for years afterward I wasn't able to publish a thing. If they even remembered, people assumed I had stopped writing or lost *the muse*, or *my voice*, or whatever it is they think we writing types need. But I didn't. I still wrote, though I no longer dropped everything else in my life for my writing, and I let my money job turn into a real job. It's amazing how far you can get if you show up for work every day and don't sound like a complete idiot when you open your mouth. I went from copyediting two days a week at *Financial World* to being its European editor, writing the stories of corporations and currencies instead of characters.

Georgie and I had by that time reached the age where you started to look at what other people were doing with their lives. Had they found what they wanted? Were they as happy as their Christmas letters sounded? What were we doing wrong? We had spent all of our twenties and most of our thirties being young and poor and artistic; now it was time to get serious. Lots of actors left the business when they reached their late thirties—they weren't getting enough work, or they had kids and didn't want to go on the road anymore, or they were really sick of how hard it all was. Equity even had an outplacement program to help them retrain. Some of Georgie's recovering actor friends had become massage therapists, real estate brokers, teachers. Georgie stuck with acting because there was nothing else she could bear to do, though fewer and fewer things had come her way once the children were born. When we had only Fergus and were still in Manhattan she worked regularly, but after the twins and the move it became increasingly hard. She had to turn down lots of work for logistical reasons—someone was sick, or paying a babysitter would use up every cent she made on the job. Sometimes it was just harder to get people to call you when your area code was no longer 212. Most of her recent work had been commercials, trade shows, some voice-overs, very little theater. She had taken only small pleasure in the work itself, laced as it always was with anxiety about being needed at home.

As for me, forty-one was an age when many men were starting to wonder how they were going to make it though twenty-five more years in jobs they already hated, but I was, in a way, just starting out. I had my first real job and I found it rewarding to do something and be good at it. I found it rewarding to get paid.

If it all sounds too easy, let me tell you, it was not. It is impossible to describe what I lost by admitting to myself and to others that my writing was not going to sell, that I was not going to be a writer, and not because of some grand unfairness in the world, some insane miscalculations on the parts of stupid editors or lazy literary agents, but just because of who I was and what I was able to do. If you give up your life's dream you relinquish the most essential part of yourself. In a way you never recover, yet you emerge from the wreckage with no choice but to start again.

In those years I had become, with an embarrassed sense of pride, mostly a businessman, and Georgie had become, mostly, a mother. Pity me for not recognizing that the path of compromise was more easily traveled by one of us than the other.

*G*eorgie had a list of People to Call in London, mostly Friends of Friends, People with Kids the Same Age, a few Theater Contacts she had collected from friends in New York, but that first day alone in London she didn't feel like calling anyone at all. She had to wait for the air shipment to arrive, and she wanted to sit in the front window of our new house and do just that: wait. The large picture window overlooked the sidewalk, and occasionally someone would pass by mere inches from where she sat in the house. The street was not heavily trafficked, but at the end of it was a row of shops—a newsagent, a wine shop, a dry cleaner, a pub—that drew local residents and the occasional delivery truck. A couple of nannies pushing baby carriages came by, and Georgie savored their lilting northern accents. She sat in the window for over an hour, loving the muffled hum of the street. It wasn't the grinding traffic and noise of Manhattan, or the soul-emptying quiet of New Jersey. It was something else, its own heedless world, a promise made for the first time, just to her.

When the movers arrived, Georgie stood on the sidewalk, telling them where to put all the boxes and bubble-wrapped parcels they carried off the truck. In the midst of the deliveries a woman came out of a mint-green house across the street and hurried over to talk to her.

"Are you just moving in?" she asked. An American accent, southern but tinged with British inflection. She had frosted blond hair and wore a strong, beautiful French perfume.

"Yes," Georgie said.

"Welcome to London," the woman said. "I'm Jean. I live at number six."

"Georgie Connolly. You're American?"

"Yes. Kensington is quite the American ghetto. There are lots of us here, you'll see. And the French, of course, because the Lycée's not far. Where are you from?"

No one but me would have heard the hesitation. "New York," Georgie said.

"Me too. Westchester. Listen, I'm on my way to French class now, but I'd love to talk to you. I can give you lots of numbers—the butcher's, a good American-style dry cleaner, a really divine cheese shop. I can save you having to do all the legwork on your own. Oh, and there's a great American women's club here with wonderful programs. Their art history course is to die for. One of the top art historians in London teaches it. I'll tell you what I can do. I can stop by when my life's not so chaotic and give you all the details. How's that?"

Jean smiled as Georgie murmured, "Thank you," and then hurried down the street, leaving Georgie with an anxious sort of disappointment that the first person she had met in London was a suburban American woman.

By the end of that first week, though, she understood what Jean meant. The nice older couple to our right were British, as were the younger, more standoffish couple to our left, but other than that everyone she met seemed to be foreign. "The English can't afford to live here anymore," Jean told Georgie when she stopped by a few days later with her brochures and lists. "Kensington is only for the super-rich or those of us on hefty expat packages." Also from Jean, whom she was beginning to dislike, Georgie learned that American wives in London were called "trailing spouses," and that none of them, it seemed, worked. Instead, they learned French or Italian, enrolled in antiques courses at Sotheby's, or signed up for day trips to pottery outlet stores.

"A day trip shopping," Georgie said to me. "What do you think? Can you just see me on that bus?"

"What about looking for work?" I asked her. "The boys are in school all day." It wasn't hard to sense her restlessness, her new faith in possibilities.

"I'm going to give it a try," she said, smiling. "As soon as the sea shipment arrives I'll have my headshots, and then I'll see what I can do."

☙

When you are early into something new the days seem full and eventful, like those of childhood. When there is no established routine even the most mundane of errands seem enchanting, if only because you're doing them against a new backdrop. For Georgie, those first weeks unfolded with sheer pleasure. She learned that because the refrigerator was so small she had to go shopping every second day, European style. She learned that the tiny washing machine in the kitchen was actually a combination washer/dryer and that after the long washing cycle was done and the water drained out, the drying cycle would begin. The machine could fit only a handful of clothes rather than an armful, but if you left it alone for three hours you would come back to clothes that were not only washed, but also dry—astonishingly wrinkled, but dry. And she learned that in England you had to have a license to watch TV. Threatening little letters kept appearing through the mail slots insisting that inspectors were lurking about and would one day arrive to slap us with a fine if they caught us watching the BBC without paying our fee.

Georgie found all these things charming rather than annoying. She was touched by the way taxi drivers would wait to make sure she was safely inside the house before driving away, she loved the big yellow signs that occasionally appeared on street corners after crimes had been committed, appealing for witnesses. "Imagine if they did that in New York," she said. "There would be a sign every three feet."

By her third week in London, Georgie felt as if she had been there for years. The house was in order, the boys were settled in school, and she was ready to work on herself.

She decided to call Graham Leggett, a British friend who had assistant-directed a show she'd done years ago in New York and who now worked as a casting director in London.

"Ah, the beautiful and desirable Georgina Connolly," he said when she reached him on the mobile number his answering machine instructed her to call.

"I'm here," she said. "I've moved to London."

"Have you, now?"

"And I'm looking for work."

"Ah," he said, "well, we have a new tradition of American actresses coming over and taking their clothes off on the London stage. Don't fancy being Mrs. Robinson, do you?"

"Ha," Georgie snorted.

"No, you are not too young, my dear," Graham said. "Anne Bancroft was thirty-six when she made the film."

"Don't even tell me that."

"What have you been in lately?"

"Some commercials, not a lot of theater. I've had these kids . . . I'm dying to get back into it."

"I don't know of anyone looking for American accents at the moment," he said dismissively.

"What about *Rent?*"

"They're supposed to be twenty, not forty."

"I'm not forty, I'm . . . thirty-nine."

"Well, then."

"God, I really am about to be forty. It sounds ravaged and inconsolable."

"As well it should," said Graham, who was past forty himself. "Have you gotten fat?"

"No."

"Wrinkled?"

"Not too. Surely there must be some Eugene O'Neill play to be cast. And you Brits are hopeless with southern accents. What about Tennessee Williams?"

"Look, let's have lunch. What does your diary look like next week?"

Georgie snorted. "Next week? What about today? What are you doing *right now?*"

"Right now?"

"Do you have plans, or are you just sitting there practicing being officious?"

He blustered.

"Just tell me where to meet you," she said. "I promise I won't tell anyone you're so unpopular I actually scheduled a lunch with you on the day."

"Thank you for that, anyway, my love."

Maybe she spent an extra minute or two looking in the mirror before she met him, maybe she patted her stomach or squinted in order to measure the breadth and depth of her crow's-feet, but she wasn't worried. She looked good and she knew it. Never an ingénue, Georgie had the kind of looks that grew more interesting with age. Despite her bold New York mannerisms, she had delicate facial features, a pretty mouth, those deep attractive wells under her eyes. People noticed her, strangers stared at her. Often it was impossible for me to take my eyes off of her.

When she walked into the Soho noodle bar to meet Graham she couldn't believe she had spent half a minute worrying about her appearance. It was he who looked toadish: paunchy, pasty, with slightly greasy hair.

Graham had gotten a lot of mileage out of his accent in New York. It had made more than one woman overlook the pastiness and single eyebrow. Shoving a script to one side, he got to his feet and kissed Georgie on the lips.

"Found something for me already?" she asked, gesturing toward the script.

"It's a disaster," he said. "This thing was cast ages ago, then the actress was offered a movie and now she's gone. Rehearsals start next month. The director's livid, the playwright's planning to decapitate me. I've got to go to them next Tuesday with some real possibilities or I'm doomed."

"What's the play?" Georgie asked.

"A new play by Piers Brighstone. A one-woman show. The life of Mrs. Jordan."

"Mrs. Who?"

"Dora Jordan? Extremely famous actress of the late eighteenth, early nineteenth century? Mistress to the Duke of Clarence, who later, of course, was to be King William the Fourth?"

"Of course," Georgie said. "Sorry, never heard of her."

"God, you Yanks."

"What's she known for, her acting or her mistressing?"

"Both. And her sorry end."

"Oh."

"But there's now my own sorry end to contemplate. It's a touring production, but it's got some London dates, and it's a Piers Brighstone play. A premiere."

Georgie's attempt not to look clueless failed.

"And you really think the Home Office should permit you to live in Britain?" Graham asked. "You have no idea who Piers Brighstone is, do you?"

"Tell me. Maybe I've heard of him, I don't know."

"Piers Brighstone. He's one of our most popular playwrights. He has an extraordinary range. His last play was set on Pluto."

"Oh," Georgie said, not at all intrigued.

"But this one's historical. And it's quite good, I think. He's a peculiar fellow, Brighstone, a bit of an institution here, really. Never workshops his stuff, never takes commissions or works with actors at festivals to develop his work. He just emerges from deepest darkest Dorset with a new play and then retreats."

"I can do English accents," Georgie persisted. "C'mon, where's she from? Yorkshire? Midlands?" She tried out her best Derbyshire: "Oh, luv, me gloves have gone missing," and "Shall I make you a nice cup o' tea?"

"It's more complicated than that." Graham said. "She was Irish, actually, but . . ."

Irish. *C'mere, lass, and sit upon me knee.* The voice of her father rose immediately in her head, filling her with that warm-edged ache that always accompanied his memory.

"Irish," she said softly. "I can definitely do Irish."

Graham was shaking his head. "Not possible. They'd never give it to an American. You have no familiarity with the character. You don't even know who she is."

"Stop being so pompous, Graham. I'll bet half the people in here don't know who this Mrs. Whatever her name—"

"Jordan."

"—Jordan is."

"Plus," Graham said, changing tacks, "it's an incredibly demanding part."

"I've done one-woman shows before," Georgie said. "I've done *Belle of Amherst*, if you want to talk about demanding."

"Emily Dickinson," Graham said. "Crazy old bat."

"Playing Emily Dickinson changed my *life*," Georgie said.

"Crazy old spinster," Graham teased.

She got nowhere with him, but as they ate, talked, caught up on the years since they'd seen each other, Georgie kept eyeing the script under his chair. *Shakespeare's Woman*, it was called.

When one of the many calls to his mobile took Graham outside, pacing and yelling and flailing his arms in front of the restaurant window, Georgie grabbed the script and stuffed it into her bag.

*L*ater that evening, the boys in bed, the two of us alone in the sitting room, she gave me my own private performance. I sat on the couch with my glass of red wine and she—dressed in jeans and a white tank top, hair in a ponytail, pink-polished toes bare—turned from the fireplace toward me and began.

Mrs Jordan: the whole of my name is a lie, a stage name if you prefer that gentler thought. I was born Dorothy Bland, but Bland is no name for the stage. I chose first to go on as Miss Francis; my father's name was Francis and I suppose that was all I could take from him. He had left my mother and the rest of us when I was young, you see, and started his new family somewhere far away.

Her tone was formal, dramatic, but after crossing the tiny sitting room in only two or three strides she smiled at me and spoke more familiarly.

My father and mother were strolling players, both of them, and that is what most of us became as well.

My parents named me Dorothy, and some have called me that, or Dorothea, though I have always preferred Dora myself. I grew up in Ireland, but I was born in London and I have always believed my birthplace left in me some seed that longed for a return. Dublin never felt like a home to me; if it were possible for the wealth of Ireland to be tied to my feet I most solemnly and seriously declare I would still not wish to encounter it again.

Here she crossed the room again, constrained by the space but using it all. She looked very pretty, and I watched with interest. She touched her belly and continued.

I departed Ireland at twenty, pregnant with the child of a Smock Alley stage manager who conceived himself entitled to command the favors of every lady in his service. I began to call myself Mrs then, the reason obvious, but most of us in the theatre went by Mrs anyway. It gave us some small measure of protection from the men in the audience who pursued us.

Eyebrows raised, she held out her arms and gave me a coy look.

And Jordan, you ask? Of course you must be curious about the origin of my second name. When I first arrived in England I started work with Tate Wilkinson's company, up in Yorkshire, and it was Tate who named me. He said, "My dear, you have crossed the water from Ireland, and so I shall call you Jordan."

She went to sit on the small settee in front of the window and seemed to gather unseen skirts around her, as if settling in for a long, old-fashioned story.

I have been called many other names in my life. Dorothea Bland. Miss Francis. Mrs Ford, when people mistakenly thought I was married to Richard Ford, who was the father of two of my girls. I have been called Mama, that dearest of names, by my lovely children, and Mrs Fitzclarence for years, when I was with the Duke. Of course I have also been called vile, horrible names by the press, by the public, during the times that they hated me, names I will not repeat for you now. During my present melancholy situation I have been calling myself Mrs James so that no one who knows Mrs Jordan will have to learn what has become of her.

Still, some do find me, as you have, admirers who learn that I stop here in this gloomy house, looking out a dirty window at an unweeded garden, with only Miss Sketchley for company.

She didn't hurry to get through her lines but sat contemplatively, gazing out the sitting room window as if she really were seeing that unpleasant garden in France. Then she called offstage—

Miss Sketchley, Miss Sketchley, please bring our guest some tea. It is so cold and we do need some English comforts.

Turning again to me she said,

Now, where was I? Oh yes, Mrs Jordan. In truth, I was never a Mrs. There were three men and thirteen children, but I was no one's bride. Two of the men would not marry me, you see, and the third was never legally permitted to do so.

Nonetheless, Mrs Jordan is who they worshipped, Mrs Jordan is the one who sold so very many tickets for so very many years, but like all the names I have used in my life, Mrs Jordan is entirely made up.

She gazed directly at me, strong clear eyes meeting mine, a hint of flirtation on her lips.

It does not matter, not really; no one seemed ever to mind. Who you are has never been important to the people in the audience.

"So what do you think?" she asked, almost without a pause, before I even knew she was finished.

"I think you're sexy," I said.

"What I mean is, would you want to see more?"

"Absolutely," I said. "Much more. Shall we move on to the lap-dance phase of the evening?"

"Stop it," she said, coming to flop next to me on the couch. All the furniture in this adorable little house seemed built to three-quarters scale, and Georgie and I were tall people. Together we filled up the couch, so she turned to one side and nested her bare feet on my lap.

"It's not supposed to be sexy," she said. "She's fifty-four years old, she's sick, miserable, swollen, and dying."

"I didn't quite get that," I teased, clasping my hand around her thick ponytail.

"You've been seduced by the intimacy of the space."

"No, I've been seduced by my gorgeous wife."

"No, the space."

"No, you."

Georgie flicked her fingernail at my arm. "She needs to seduce, but not in a sexual way. What she really needs is to command the audience."

"Is that the whole play? Just standing there and talking to the audience?"

"She's talking to a visitor, this sort of fan person, Miss Williams, telling her the story of her life. It's a common thing in one-actor shows, a contrived audience, an occasion for the monologue. So, really, what do you think?"

"Are you talking to me the husband or me the audience?" I asked.

"You the esteemed theater critic for the *Times*." She laughed.

"Hmm," I said, "London or New York?"

"Both," she said, leaning over to kiss me. "Watch me," she said, sitting up. "It gets even better."

Just then a cry of "Mom mom mom *Mom*" reached us from the boys' room.

Georgie looked stricken.

"I'll go," I said.

"Thanks," she said. "I'm so into this. I really don't want to stop." She sprang from the couch to take her place in the center of the room again as I started upstairs.

Tate Wilkinson gave me my name and he also gave me my first job in England. He did not want to at first, but I do understand that. I had arrived from Ireland with my mother, my sister Hester and brother George, all of us looking for work in the theatre. I had no money, no clothes, not a friend in all of England, and a baby on the way. Tate may not have thought much of me, but he was a kind soul, perhaps the kindest I have ever encountered in the theatre, and with some reluctance he finally agreed to let me speak some lines for him.

To this day I do not know why, Miss Williams, but I chose to recite from The Fair Penitent, *that tragedy of rape. It is a part I had never played before, but the plight of Calista was almost identical to my own. I read some of her lines, after she is seduced by Lothario:*

Oh! Let me hear no more; I cannot bear it,
'Tis deadly to remembrance; let that night, that guilty night,
* be blotted from the year;*
Let not the voice of mirth, or musick, know it.
Let it be dark and desolate; no stars to glitter o'er it; let it wish
* for light,*
Yet want it still, and vainly want the dawn;
For 't was the night that gave me up to shame,
To sorrow, to perfidious, false Lothario.

I had chosen perfectly, you see; how much I looked the part. I held nothing back, and if I shocked Tate a little, I also delighted him. His misgivings melted away.

Because I had read from tragedy he asked me if that was my prefer- ence, or rather comedy or opera or farce. Immediately I answered, "All," and honestly, I never saw an elderly gentleman more astonished.

Georgie did not move from the sitting room all night, going through the script, line by line, while upstairs I ministered to Fergus, who was having obsessive nighttime thoughts about the sewer system. When Graham called later that night, looking for the script, Georgie's great love affair with Dora Jordan had already begun.

"If you want it back, you're going to have to let me read for it," she told him.

"Jesus Christ, Georgie, don't be an idiot. I need that script. I've got notes all over it."

"Some of them pretty misguided, from what I can see."

"Look, I'm going to lose my last shred of credibility with the playwright if I have to ask him for another copy. I'm coming over straightaway to collect it."

"I've got it all figured out," Georgie said. "Don't tell them I'm American. Tell them I'm Irish. I'm half Irish, you know. My dad insisted we all have dual citizenship. I'll flash my Irish passport."

"Irish? That's even worse," Graham said. "Besides, I'm not lying to these people. Let's just be vaguely noncommittal."

"Oh let's," Georgie said. "Vague is okay. I can be vague."

"All right Georgie, for fuck's sake. E-mail me a photo and I'll put you up for it. But you're going last."

"I'll go last."

"And I'm going to murder you after."

"Fine. Murder me after. But let me read first."

And so, while I had fallen asleep on Fergus's bed, answering his terrified questions about pipes and drains and where does the poo and pee go, Georgie sat up alone all night in the sitting room, devouring the script.

Perhaps I had made such a strong impression as Calista that he was unable to see me as anything else, for when Tate asked me to join his company it was The Fair Penitent we rehearsed and performed first. We began in Leeds, and later that winter went to York, then Hull and Sheffield. Every week I looked more and more the part.

There were thirty of us in Tate's company. We were not well known then, but many of us became so. The Lengs, the Cumminses, the Parnells, the comedian Mr. Creswell, George Inchbald—some very famous names, Miss Williams, surely you have heard of many of them?

The Yorkshire circuit was not easy for us. We traveled on foot and occasionally on horse from town to town all through that cold winter, taking lodging near the theatre and rehearsing until Tate was satisfied. When we were performing, we went on each evening from six until midnight. I played any and every part: no sooner had I closed the tragedy by my supposed death than I put on a frock and mob cap and ran back upon the stage to warble "The Greenwood Laddie."

It was in Hull, in November, that my little girl was born, just before my twenty-first birthday. I named her Frances, but have called her Fanny ever since.

I stayed in the straw for several weeks, but Tate wanted me to go on as Calista on Boxing Day. A terrible mistake. The people of Leeds and York had tolerated me as I grew bigger, but in Hull, now that they knew I had a child, they tried to hiss me from the stage. I would not leave. I have never in my career, Miss Williams, left the stage. I finished my performance each and every night while Tate worked to end the gossip in the town. Within weeks I had won over the people of Hull, and there were sellouts from then on. I believe the actress in me helped close their eyes to what they despised about the woman.

I spent three years with Tate's company, three years dragging my daughter about the moors, lodging in homes where we were nearly devoured by bugs, keeping Fanny backstage in the theatre with me as I rehearsed and performed. It was a hard life, and after I built my reputation I was ready to get out of the provinces. Some advised me against venturing on the London boards, insisting I was better off where I was than acting second parts in tragedies in London. Nevertheless, an offer of four pounds a week came from London, and with Tate's blessing, I took Fanny and my *mother, sister, and brother with me in a public coach for the two-day journey to the capital.*

❧

The next morning, I found Georgie in last night's chair, the gas fire going, the script on her lap. She had read all through the night.

"The poor woman," she told me. "She had thirteen children, but she died completely alone, and penniless, in France."

"At least it was France," I said.

"Her daughter's husband was stealing from her, running up debts in her name. She feared she'd be arrested, so she decided to go abroad while things were sorted out. She had no one to help her, she didn't know what to do."

"And she just died there?"

Georgie nodded vigorously. "An obscure little town called St. Cloud. It's all here, the whole story of her life. It's one of the most fascinating things I've ever read. I can't believe I've never even *heard* of her before. She was phenomenally famous—the Angelina Jolie of her time. Her lover was a son of George the Third. William, Duke of Clarence. He went on to become the king of England himself after his brother, George the Fourth, died."

"Did you read the whole thing?" I asked, and she nodded.

"Jesus, Georgie."

"I know," she said, and I had the first inkling of how much she loved this part. People always assume actors are well-read, but Georgie could barely tolerate reading. She had a mild form of dyslexia that had gone undiagnosed in her childhood, and as a result she found reading extremely difficult and exhausting. Reading a script for the first time was normally torture for her, but as compensation, she had a formidable memory. When she did a play she was able to quickly master not only her own lines but everyone else's as well.

I looked at her there, wrapped in an afghan, clutching a cup of tea long grown cold, her face tired but beautiful, as I had seen it many times after she sat up all night when one of the boys was sick. I leaned down and kissed her.

"I've got to get this part, Peter," she said against my cheek. "I've got to go in there and just nail it."

"You will," I said.

There's no better fantasy than the part not yet won, the book just begun, the song that is only two bars of music playing in your head as you walk through the city. Never is it easier to catapult yourself to the Tonys, the Grammys, the National Book Awards dinner. That's where Georgie was with Mrs. Jordan, and I envied her for that.

She dragged us all up to some manor house in Buckinghamshire to look at a portrait of Mrs. Jordan in one of her most famous roles. *The Country Girl*—an innocent young thing in a sweet white dress and blue sash. She spent three-quarters of an hour in front of the painting while the boys ran wild, were chastised by the museum guard, and eventually sent to play in the garden in the rain.

After seeing the painting, Georgie decided that the dress was the key to Mrs. Jordan, and to the audition. She bought meters and meters of filmy white fabric and for a very motivating fee persuaded Hortensia, the cleaning woman, to copy the *Country Girl* dress and sew it almost overnight.

She chose a risky scene for the audition—Dora's meteoric rise to fame, Dora as the toast of the London theater world—and she rehearsed it endlessly.

On the day of the audition, she strolled down the street in that dress, thankful that none of the neighbors was around to see. She couldn't get on the tube like that, so she hailed a taxi instead.

The theater wasn't in the West End, but in an edgy part of northwest London, and she realized how ridiculous she looked, standing on the street corner, paying the taxi driver. She hadn't wanted to crush the dress by wearing a coat over it, but it was a blustery day, and cold, and she was freezing. Grit from the street blew in her eyes, the wind pinned a striped plastic bag against the long white skirt.

Graham was waiting for her inside. "Look at you," he said. "Oh my, the girls in their summer dresses."

"Is there a bathroom?" she asked.

At the mirror over the sink she repaired the wind's damage to her hair and retied the sash of the dress to make it fresh. Her cheeks were flushed, her eyes tearing; she hoped she looked vibrant instead of stressed.

"It hasn't been going well," Graham told her when she rejoined him. "They've been seeing people all day and haven't found anyone they like. Bad news for me but it could be good for you. There's no one in there right now. Just the playwright and the director and their collective despair."

The theater was small and slightly cramped, with seats on three sides of the stage, but Graham called it "a proper theater," with plush red velvet seats—no black risers and folding chairs. Georgie immediately loved the intimacy of the space. It seemed to be a continuation of the small sitting room in our house, where she had been rehearsing.

A man and a woman sitting side by side in the third row stood up as Georgie approached. Graham gestured toward the woman.

"The director, Nicola Deane," Graham said. Nicola was a small, dark-haired woman, about Georgie's age, with intense eyes and sharp features. She looked tired, Georgie noticed, slightly annoyed, and her mechanical smile faded as quickly as it had been summoned.

"Georgie Connolly," Georgie said, speaking quickly, trying not to give away her accent.

The man gave Georgie a wide smile and held out his hand. "Piers Brighstone," he said. Thin, tanned, and silver-haired, he had the look of an aging rock star, though perhaps without so many drugs in his past. He was clearly older than Georgie—in his early fifties, she guessed—and he wore a faded jean jacket over a black T-shirt. She had planned to mumble so as not to give away her accent, but he was so recklessly gorgeous she found she couldn't say anything to him anyway. She managed to hold out her hand and he said, "Pleasure," with great gusto as she stared into his serene blue eyes.

Nicola was looking at Georgie's dress with amusement, and Georgie suddenly felt like Vivien Leigh trying to win the part of Scarlett O'Hara. Piers, however, eyed the dress with great interest, his smile steady, a boyish sort of delight on his face. Graham hurried her toward the stage, discouraging chat, and Georgie was grateful for that. It would not be any witty small talk or eager self-promotion that would win her this part, she knew. If she were to be chosen, it would be solely because the remarkable Mrs. Jordan had chosen to speak through her.

She felt Piers's eyes follow her as she walked, and that appreciative, interested gaze gave her the last measure of confidence she needed to go on.

Less than a year after I arrived in London, my portrait hung in the Royal Academy. To say that my success was instant may be immodest, but there it is.

Hoppner painted me as Comedy herself; I held Comedy's mask in my hand. He titled the painting Mrs Jordan as the Comic Muse Supported by Euphrosyne, Who Represses the Advances of a Satyr. *I detest that ugly satyr, but we do not all require genius to understand who he is. I saw the way men looked at me from the audience. Do they not know how easy it is for an actress to tell what they are thinking?*

All of London came to see the painting. It was as large as Reynolds' painting of Mrs Siddons as the Tragic Muse. Everyone said that Mrs Siddons represented Tragedy, while I was the personification of Comedy.

Perhaps it is only I who find it strange that I began my career in England as Calista and then became best known, best loved, for my comic parts. My Rosalind, my Hippolita, my Country Girl. My friend Peter Pindar even had a little rhyme:

Had Shakespeare's self at Drury been
While Jordan plays each varied scene
He would have started from his seat
And cried—"That's Rosalind complete."

Everyone wished to paint Mrs Jordan in those days. My picture was in all the print-shop windows. Whoever said I was just a strolling player? Soon I was to become the Duchess of Drury Lane.

Romney painted me in his studio at Cavendish Square. He usually charged eighty guineas for a portrait, but for me there was no fee. Do not deceive yourself that he found it an honor to paint me. He may have been the most famous portrait artist of his time, but he was also a shrewd busi-nessman. He knew he could earn his money back several times over by selling copies of my picture.

He painted me in my costume from The Country Girl, *a white dress with a blue sash tied in a bow on the side, my hair tumbling wildly. It was my most popular role. Do you know it, Miss Williams? She's an innocent nineteen-year-old:*

> *Pray, sister, where are the best fields and woods to walk in, in London?*

It should have been a pleasure to paint me as the Country Girl, but he was a difficult man, Romney, a bit moody and suspicious. He did not like any of the poses I suggested, and his own ideas were uninspiring to me.

I have no patience for vanity and so finally I ran toward the door and glanced back to tell him I was leaving—just like this, my hands up almost in prayer position, my head thrown back, curls tumbling down my shoulders.

"Yes," he cried, "that will do," and it was in this way I pretended he had discovered the pose I knew all along to be very fetching, the pose that always has its intended effect.

Romney made a fortune from that painting.

I do not know what your experience has been in these instances, Miss Williams, but I find it better sometimes to let the men believe they are the ones who have made the important discoveries. Most especially the men who are artists.

It wasn't an easy choice for an audition; there weren't many who would have been able to pull the scene off. There was an obvious way to do it—all gay self-intoxication—but Georgie tried what she came to think of as a certain cunning naïveté. She wanted to capture Dora's charm and wonderment and sheer delight without letting it escalate into arrogance or vanity.

She ended the scene in the middle of the empty stage, now an artist's studio she had created with her body, her voice, and gesture. She kept her gaze clear and direct, trained on the writer and director, unable to wait even a moment to know what they thought. It needed to knock their socks off, that scene, it needed to win her the part, and it appeared that it did. Piers looked avid, somewhat beaming, as if he wanted to jump onto the stage and congratulate her, though Georgie thought she saw Nicola put her hand on his arm and mouth the word *Wait*.

Little was said after she finished; they told her they would let her know in a week or so. As soon as she got home, Georgie cried her heart out like a teenager who had done everything in her power to impress a boy at a party and then found him kissing another girl on the coats in the bedroom.

She hadn't thought about not getting the part.

"I think I'll die," she said when she called to tell me about the audition. "I know I've wanted things this badly before and not gotten them, but I can't do that again. I've had that experience. This time I need to get it. How in hell am I going to wait a whole week?"

But she didn't need to wait. Graham called that evening, and when she turned from the phone she let out a whoop so loud that I could hear her over Liam's and Fergus's battling, so loud that Jack came upstairs from his time-out in the kitchen to find out what had happened.

"Mommy got a job," she said.

"Mommy got a job, Mommy got a job," three boys chanted, beginning to jump and dance and hug her wildly. She picked up Liam, then Jack, and danced around the room, nearly falling over in that small sitting room. They didn't really know what was happening, but in their mother's face was an expression they had never seen before, and one that I could recall only dimly, an expression both beguiling and beguiled. She was falling in love with her life again, and it was for that they danced.

*I*t felt then like the beginning of a charmed life. Or, perhaps the beginning for the boys and me, but a sequel for Georgie. In my opinion, she had always led a charmed life.

She was raised in Greenwich Village, in a blue brick townhouse on Hudson Street, a hundred-and-fifty-year-old building with sloping wood floors and pressed-tin ceilings that got lower and lower the closer you got to the roof. On Saturday mornings, the smell of perm solution from the first-floor beauty parlor rose acridly to the top of the house and stuck in Georgie's bedroom.

Georgie's father was an Irishman; her mother had met him on a cruise she took to celebrate her graduation from Barnard. The bird-like Pearl, as I've come to refer to Georgie's mother, was a Renaissance Studies major with an interest in painting. Fergus, Georgie's father, was coming across to work in his uncle's construction business. This was in 1959. Things in the west of Ireland were as bad as they'd ever been—which is to say pretty awful—and Fergus was happy to try his luck in Manhattan. In fact, he had a damned fine time.

After he and Pearl married, they rented two small rooms in that house on Hudson Street, and as the babies came they took over more and more of the building until they could afford to buy it outright. They might just as easily have moved to New Jersey or one of the Long Island South Shore towns, but why move? The White Horse Tavern was two blocks away, and times were prosperous. Fergus built up a loyal clientele, young couples who turned out to be upwardly mobile and who would let no one but him touch their kitchen remodeling job or their new bathroom. Georgie and her three older brothers grew up on the streets of the Village, went to the local public school and the magnet high schools. Georgie loved her childhood, the school year in Manhattan, summers at her grandfather's farm in the west of Ireland, all green fields and sheep.

She was a New Yorker, born and bred, and in a sense I, coming to New York from central Illinois at the advanced age of twenty-six, never quite caught up. I was in thrall to the city and to the woman it gave me.

"My dad would never have left," she told me the night we moved from Manhattan to New Jersey. She lay on a mattress on the floor of our new bedroom, crying, three babies in the next room, in my arms but more lonely than she had ever been in her life. I held her tightly, wiping at her tears with my pillowcase, stroking her hair until she seemed to be asleep. I then pulled away gently, and just as my own breathing became even and I began to cross over to sleep, I heard her say quietly, "My life. My life is over."

We had had no choice but to leave. We couldn't afford a bigger place in Manhattan and there was no way we could raise three boys there on our income, so we had moved to the suburbs, to the town everybody tells themselves is the Upper West Side transplanted, and learned, like everybody else, that we couldn't fool ourselves into thinking that was so.

Though I had hoped Georgie would adapt to what I saw as an easy suburban life, in the four years we lived in New Jersey, she never did. It was more than a year before she made a single friend. Her real life was in the city, and sometimes she took the boys into New York for the day for no discernible reason, just to walk around. She belonged in the city; like the old man on the mountain, that was her place in the world, and we should have done anything we could to stay. Easy to see in hindsight, but also easy to feel that, in another great city, on another continent, I was erasing her four years of unhappiness and setting her charmed life back on course.

*I*n the two weeks before rehearsals began, Georgie interviewed a dozen nannies, trying to find the one she could imagine picking the boys up from school each day, patiently helping them with their homework, making them dinner, and, if necessary, gently putting them to bed.

London nannies were different from the gum-snapping Megans and Katies who had babysat for us in New Jersey, fourteen- and fifteen-year-olds with shiny ponytails and soccer shorts, girls who seemed to answer every question with a peppy "Not a problem."

Here there were Sarahs and Emmas and Janes with pierced eyebrows or belly buttons, midriff tops and tattoos at the base of their spines. They seemed as if they had been around, and many of them had; most were from Australia or New Zealand, here to work and see Europe. A lot of them were in transit and wouldn't commit to a defined period of time. Georgie needed someone who would stay. Someone who would be flexible enough to change her schedule as Georgie moved from daytime rehearsals to evening performances to going on the road with the show. She finally decided to hire a girl who had a boyfriend, thinking that might help keep her around for a while.

And so we suddenly had Emma, a large and kindhearted twenty-year-old from Yorkshire who looked strong enough to withstand the knuckleheaded behavior of three small boys.

The boys didn't know what to make of Emma.

"I don't want a nanny," Liam told Georgie. He told Emma he didn't like her and would pour apple juice and orange juice on her.

"Don't worry, he'll forget about it," Jack said, climbing into Emma's lap.

"But how will she know what to make us for dinner?" asked Fergus, our worrier. "How will she find our school? What if I need you and only her is there?"

Emma just laughed. On her first day of work she brought a notebook and asked Fergus to draw a picture of everything he didn't like to eat. This made Fergus feel important, and he got to work immediately.

"Do you know I don't like bananas?" he asked her as he drew. "Do you know Jack likes cut-up apples and me apples not cut up and Liam never apples at all?"

It amazed us that we had a nanny. In New Jersey, money had been so tight that we could afford a babysitter only once in a while, mostly to go to the movies or occasionally into Manhattan to see a friend of Georgie's in a show. Most of the time we played tag team at the train station, with me hopping off the train and into the driver's seat while Georgie kissed the boys goodbye and caught the next train back into the city. On these occasions she would pass me a tight-lipped kiss and some grim fact, such as: "Did you know that a woman's life is shortened by thirty-four weeks for each boy baby she gives birth to? Do you know what that means? I've already lost two whole years." Or: "I've got to stop these evenings out. They interfere with my career as a laundress."

When she said things like that I would give her a good-natured midwestern smile of complicity because I wanted to be sympathetic and unconnected to all she claimed was ruining her life. I didn't argue, didn't point out, *But look what you have,* just sympathized with her for all she had given up.

I believe that was one of the places I started to lose my footing in our marriage. Shouldn't I have told her she was acting spoiled, selfish, that everyone's life had flat, ordinary parts? That growing older meant moving on, closing chapters in your life and opening new ones—all the things my parents had taught me and I had wordlessly accepted?

Perhaps my inability to say anything cruel to her—*Well, anytime you want to earn enough money to hire a housekeeper, be my guest*—my tendency to always be on her side, the fact that I loved her too much, made her feel she could do what she wanted in our marriage.

And yet had she known what was going to happen to her, to us, I know she would gladly have traded each moment of passion for decades of the tedium she then so fiercely attacked.

*H*er obsession with Mrs. Jordan only grew once she had the part.

It wasn't just the script, over and over and over again, though there was that. She read biographies and journals, studies of eighteenth-century theater, books about royalty and politics and war. After dropping the boys off at school, she rode the tube to museums to look at paintings of Mrs. Jordan; she wandered Drury Lane and Covent Garden, sometimes standing still with closed eyes to imagine what it was like when Mrs. Jordan was there.

She went to Buckingham Palace to view Hoppner's painting of Mrs. Jordan as the Comic Muse, but what moved her more was a statue she discovered in the lobby of the Picture Gallery—a statue of Mrs. Jordan and two of her children. It had been commissioned by Dora's lover, the Duke, after he became king of England. This was years after Dora's death, years and years after the Duke had dumped her. He had begun collecting paintings of her and wanted a statue as well. He felt guilty for his bad behavior, perhaps, or wanted to honor the mother of his children. Some might argue that his motives were true regret and real love. Whatever his reasons, the statue's commission was one of his first official acts after his coronation as William IV, and he wept as he told the sculptor, Francis Chantrey, exactly what he wanted. He meant for the sculpture to be placed in Westminster Abbey, but because of Mrs. Jordan's social position, the church never allowed it.

It was a beautiful statue, white marble, life-size. Chantrey had never known Mrs. Jordan and had begun the statue fifteen years after her death, but to Georgie it was the truest representation of Dora she had been able to find. Apparently the Duke was definite about what he wanted, for while most of the paintings depicted Mrs. Jordan the actress, in costume and in character, this statue was clearly meant to represent the woman.

In the statue, Mrs. Jordan sat with a baby cradled in her arms and a small boy leaning comfortably on her knees. Her long curly hair fell loosely to one side of her neck, her shoulders were almost bare, and the fabric of her gown was pulled down low, revealing the top of one breast. Her attention was wholly on her children, her gaze more tender and intimate than anything Georgie had ever seen in marble.

Dora and the baby both carried the dreamy expressions of a mother and child just finished with nursing. Next to Dora's bare and sensuous feet, half hidden by her gown, were the symbols of her profession: the mask of comedy and the lute of poetry and music.

*B*y the time of the first rehearsal, everyone knew Georgie was American, but she teased them with her best outer-borough accent anyway: *Hey guys, how ya doin'?* They were all English; they remained unfazed.

Georgie had always loved first rehearsals—meeting the other actors and deciding what she thought of the director's choices. With *Shakespeare's Woman* there were no other actors to meet, not even an understudy, because the run was so short and the part so demanding they had decided to chance it without one. Everybody else was there—Nicola and Piers and the show's producers, the stage manager, all the designers, the dialect coach, even the dresser and wig fixer.

"Don't worry," Nicola told Georgie. "I've only brought everybody in today just to meet you—they won't all stay."

Nicola was professional and pleasant, even gracious, but there was something steely underneath it all. She wore blood-red lipstick that stayed on for hours without needing refreshing, hinting to Georgie that other aspects of her character might be equally unrelenting. And Piers—

Piers.

I need to say now what I know is true: Georgie found him attractive from the very first day she saw him. The very first moment. His open face, the deep laugh lines around his eyes, the way he studied her as if she were already his—he was very appealing to her, this man who was there to ruin our lives. Because he was older, he made her feel nervous, girlish even, the way you might feel talking to the dad of someone you'd just smoked pot with. His name sounded all wrong in her American accent, the vowels too nasal, the *r* impossible for her to touch on as lightly as the British did. She was unable to say "Piers" without blushing, and she felt somewhat like a child around him, looking to him for approval from the first day onward.

"We're all very anxious to work with you," he said, by which I believe he meant *I*.

The set designer presented his plans for a simple but rich set, one with only a few pieces of big, decorous furniture. The play was set in the house in France where Dora died, but with no set changes, he explained, just clever lighting, a chair moved from here to there, the stage could easily become a dressing room, the Duke's drawing room, the stage of a play Mrs. Jordan was performing.

"We're going to go with a fair few costume changes," Susie, the costume designer, said when it was her turn. "Not complete changes, all of them. It could be a wig or a coat or an entire dress you're stepping into. We'll try to keep the changes smooth, but it's going to be demanding."

Nicola said, "We thought for a while about an understated white-linen-suit approach, the bare stage—"

"God, no," Georgie said. "That wouldn't be about Mrs. Jordan at all. People came to see her as the Country Girl, or Viola, or Rosalind.

That's who she was, and that's how we've got to present her on the stage."

"We've had quite a bit of back-and-forth on this," Nicola said, glancing at Piers. "You wouldn't believe how dignified and effective a white linen suit can be, but yes, we've come to that same conclusion, Georgie. We're going to do all of the costume changes onstage. You're going to have to learn how to carry on with your lines while stepping into a new skirt or putting on a feathered hat and jodhpurs."

Georgie nodded. "That's good," she said. "It will help the audience transition with her."

Nicola's red lips pursed so tightly they almost disappeared. "Anne will be onstage with you the whole time," she said, indicating the dresser, an impossibly young and bright-eyed girl with two long blond braids. "She will assist you with the changes, bring you your props, but she's not a character. You won't look at her. She won't be Miss Williams, and she certainly won't be Miss Sketchley. When you address Miss Williams, you address the audience, and Miss Sketchley will remain offstage."

This was the beginning of what Georgie loved most about acting in plays. Seeing the words she had fallen in love with on the page become theatrical. Taking a playwright's vision for a character and turning it into something real.

After the first hour of introductions and presentations, everybody left but Georgie, Nicola, and Piers, that triptych of actor/director/ writer that was to fill each rehearsal. Nicola, the director, wanted to do a straight reading of the play, and Georgie began in a chair with the script in front of her, but before long she was up moving about, saying her lines from different parts of the stage.

"Let's just get the words out on the stage first," Nicola said. "We'll worry about the blocking later."

"I'm not blocking it," Georgie said. "It's just instinct. My body's telling me where on the stage the words belong."

Is there any post today, Miss Sketchley?

What, none?

None at all?

Well, then, you must go again.

Oh, Miss Williams, you cannot believe what a day's post used to bring—the notes from admirers, the letters of adoration, plays and poetry dedicated to me. I have saved some all these years. I have a bundle somewhere in my desk. Where can it be?

Oh, look, here's something. A young playwright, Mr. George Saville Carey, wrote a play for me. The Dupes of Fancy, *he called it, and the frontispiece carries my picture. You must hear his dedication:*

"The tutelary sisters, Melpomene and Thalia, who preside over all the Scenic Arts, have taken you by the hand and placed you on a pedestal so high, that envy lowers her scowling front whene'er she casts her jaundiced Eye upon your exalted Station, for you justly assimulate the pathetic manners of the one, and fascinate with the bewitching archness of the other."

Is that you down there, Miss Williams? I can barely see you from the top of this pedestal.

I suppose he hoped such flattery would persuade me to act his play. Alas, I must assure you it did not.

I gained a new admirer at that time, and an important one: William, the Duke of Clarence, the king's third son. He began to pursue me with great persistence and indeed I had a letter from him nearly every day.

I did not know what to do about him.

He believed me to be married, as almost everyone did at that time, and I found it wise to let him. Richard Ford and I had been together for several years and people assumed we were truly married. Indeed I had taken to calling myself Dorothy Ford; I signed my letters so.

Yet we were not married. Richard promised marriage once or I would not have moved into Gower Street with him, but he never found it convenient to make good on that promise. I asked him many times for a definitive answer but he would not give me one. Richard's sights were on Parliament and for that reason a marriage to an actress was not advisable for him. He shrank from it.

Richard and I had two little girls together, Dodee and Lucy, and we lost a son. Richard doted on the girls, especially Dodee, but if our dear baby boy had lived, it might have made a difference. A son and heir was important to a man like Richard. I have a portrait of Richard still. I kept it for my girls. Here it is, Miss Williams. Richard was a kind man, and intelligent. You can see it in his face.

But the Duke, the ardent Duke. He made me laugh. He enjoyed his life so, and helped me to enjoy my life, and my profession, more than I had ever been able to do.

And the Duke pursued me.

After some time, I told Richard that my mind was made up: if he could think me worthy of being his wife, no temptation would be strong enough to detach me from him and my duties. But if he could not offer me that, and I must choose between offers of protection rather than marriage, I would certainly choose what promised the fairest.

By the end of the scene, Georgie stood at the center of the stage looking over her shoulder into the audience. Though the director had finally stopped telling her not to "leap about" the stage, Georgie could still sense her disapproval.

But the writer was smiling.

The writer was smiling.

Because she could not say his name without blushing, he now became the Writer when she needed to think or speak of him.

*L*eaving the theater was always a shock—out on the street again, the down-at-heels Kilburn High Road, pound shops, off-licenses, Indian takeouts. Georgie would walk to the tube, litter gusting around her legs, again as modern and urban as the street, but with a lingering wistfulness for Georgian England.

The Friday evening after her first full week of rehearsal, she went directly from the theater to have dinner with me. I came to her from what in New York is called "Wall Street," in Chicago "the Loop," and in London "the City"—in other words, the financial district, where I had been working all these weeks, getting to know the people who would make my job easier or harder, becoming *Pi-ta Maaaah-tin*, which I infinitely preferred to the broad midwestern *Pee-der Marr-din* I had embodied for most of my life.

The shape of the inner London tube is a sort of gin bottle tipped on its side, the yellow Circle line forming its outline, the Metropolitan and City lines giving it depth, all the rest of the lines feeding into or through the bottle intricately from all parts of London. Georgie came from northwest London on the silver thread that was the Jubilee line, the only line that intersected at some point with every other line in the system. I came on the pink thread from the City, watching the stops go by, studying all the stations on the tube map, marveling at the names. West Ham and East Ham. Gallions Reach. Tooting Broadway. Shoreditch. Chancery Lane. Most of these places were completely unknown to me, and so I infused them with whimsy or drama; there was a part of me that wished to change my route so that I could get off in the cool November air at Cockfosters, or Highbury, or Pudding Mill Lane instead, and see what those places meant in London, see what greeted me at the top of the stairs.

I had been the same way in New York. What if my subway stop had been Spring Street instead of Seventy-ninth Street? How would my life be different if that were my corner instead of this? I wanted to know, had always wanted to know, how one set of variables replaced with another would produce for me a different life. A childhood lived on a ranch in Montana, a California beach, or, like Georgie, a New York City townhouse. A different college, a spectacularly interesting roommate, a first job in a different city; how mightily could these changes act upon my life? I would obsess over my possible paths even while enjoying the one I was on, and every time I changed my life I wondered how the interrupted routes left behind would play out without me.

I wondered: Is the obsessive preoccupation with the road not taken peculiarly American, or only peculiarly mine? It was why Georgie had become an actress, I suspected, and why I had become a writer: to console ourselves for what we saw as the paltry single life we were given to live.

My path and Georgie's—these chosen ones, the particular paths of this evening—were careening closer to each other, her silver path and my pink. My distance was farther but hers took longer, and I arrived first at the restaurant in Marylebone Lane. I was given a corner table and, as always, chose to sit with my back to the wall, where I could see most of the tables as well as the door. Drinking my gin and tonic, I loved watching everyone who came and went or lingered at the window to look at the menu, deciding whether to come inside, but most of all I loved waiting for Georgie to arrive.

When she did arrive, she changed the whole shape of the room for me. I had become accustomed over the years to seeing my wife peripherally, by my side in a room—an ear, half a nose, a bit of a smile, an arm around me. The room always seemed to open up for us; we were the place where it began. Now she came in, and it was the whole woman confronting me.

"Georgie-girl," I said.

"Peter," she said, kissing me. Radiant. Just jeans and a pale pink sweater, but she was warm and there was a shine to her skin. She had put on fresh makeup, a spray of perfume. She didn't look at all as if she had been struggling in rehearsal all day.

But, "She's making my life *hell*," were her next words.

"Nicola?"

"Nicola? Yes, Nicola." The eyes danced. It wasn't serious. Mostly it was the joy at actually having a director to make her life hell again, the privilege of working again. "She stands so damned close to me on the stage," Georgie said. "I keep wanting to say, 'This is a one-woman show, remember?' I was feeling a little tired today—after five hours of rehearsal you'd think I'd be entitled—but no, she snaps, 'You're playing every single part exactly the same.'" Georgie delivered this last line in a sort of British Wicked Witch of the West voice.

"God, is that how she really sounds?" I asked.

"I don't even know anymore. I'm up there and I hear her voice, this nonstop commentary in my ear: 'Do it this way—no, not that way—oh, you've fucked up again.' So it's not even my normal life I have to get out of my head before I can get into the character. You know, the boys"—and here she began to imitate Liam—"'Mom, why can't I have a ja-uice box? I really want a ja-uice box'"—and Fergus—"'If there's an upstairs toilet, why doesn't the poo and pee go downstairs before it goes into the sewer system?' You know, I have to find a way to get rid of her voice as well as all the boys' before I can work my way into Mrs. Jordan, and it's exhausting even before I say the first line."

"So you and Nicola aren't on your way to becoming best girl-friends, then?" I asked.

"Honestly, Peter, she's smart as a whip, but I think she—no, I *know* she sees this character completely differently than I do."

"That's not totally unusual, is it?"

"No, but instead of trying to use the energy that comes from our differences she just wants to make me do everything her way."

"Maybe she's a frustrated actress," I said. "Maybe she wanted the part for herself."

"You may be right," she said. "I'd love to know. I'm just disappointed, I guess. I mean, a woman director, almost exactly my age, it should be this great partnership, not some sort of reverent apprentice-ship. And the Writer . . ." Her voice raised, she gave me a comic look to let me know how much she was exaggerating, and how much she enjoyed it. "*He* says nothing. He sits there, taking all these notes. I keep expecting rewrites, but there are none. Everything he's writing is about me, not the play, what I should say faster or slower or for comic effect or, for God's sake, *not* for comic effect. At the beginning of each rehearsal Nicola says, 'Piers has a few things,' and reads them off like an instruction manual. What I want to know is how he tells her all this stuff. I mean, do they have secret meetings after I leave? Does he send her e-mails, and if so, why doesn't he just e-mail me?"

"Is he shy?" I asked.

"Shy?" Georgie said the word as if it never occurred to her. "I don't know. I'm starting to think he and Nicola are lovers. I mean, they don't act lovey-dovey, but there's something . . . you know, it's weird. With anybody else I would say, 'Hey, are you two sleeping together or what?' but with them it would be, I don't know, indecorous or something. Like they're my parents."

"Your stage parents."

"Exactly," she said. "He's slightly less withholding than she is, but they're both . . . Who would name their baby 'Piers,' anyway? Who could call 'Piers' after their toddler and expect him to respond? You know what I think, I think he was never a baby at all. I think he just hatched as a brooding middle-aged playwright."

The waitress arrived. "Are you all right there?" she asked.

"We're fine," Georgie said. "Why shouldn't we be?"

"She means are we ready to order," I said.

"Sorry, we haven't even looked at the menus," Georgie said, "and we haven't even started on *his* life." The waitress smiled, not quite getting it.

"I'll have another," I said, indicating my glass. "Unless you want to order a bottle of wine?" I asked Georgie.

She frowned and shook her head. I could rarely coax Georgie into joining me for a drink. She was the token teetotaler in her large family of men who could hold their drink, and she occasionally transferred her scorn for them onto me.

When the waitress left, Georgie turned to me. "Okay," she said, smiling slyly, "Tell me. I had thirteen children, eight miscarriages, and three lovers today, and then I died. What about you?"

"I had a rough day too," I said, and we both laughed.

"Do you love it, Peter? Tell me. Do you love your new job?" She leaned toward me, eager to catch my response, as if it could be the most enchanting thing she would hear all night. She made me want to love my new job and tell her about it with as much fervor as she had for hers. And so I talked to her about the coworkers I was slowly getting to know, the trip I would need to make to Zurich the next week and Paris the week after, the New York management who would be coming in a few weeks to assess what I was doing. Because my job was new, and I was doing everything for the first time, it seemed almost as thrilling to talk about as her job. Who knew how interesting any of it really was, but Georgie was dynamic, so alive, that for the first time in a very long while I could imagine the people around us lowering their voices in order to overhear what we had to say.

"Would you look at us," I said. "We're sitting here, eating artistically arranged appetizers and gazing in each other's eyes." I reached for her hands, the perfect temperature of her flesh. It was just the two of us, on a date. How beautiful she looked, how I wanted to go home with her and avoid the house, the boys, the babysitter, and just have her.

But she had already moved on to the boys. "I love it, Peter," she said. "I really do. But I miss them so much I can't tell you—it feels as if I've handed them over to a wet nurse or something."

"You've got Mrs. Jordan on the brain."

"No, she didn't even do that. She fed them herself, kept them with her backstage, in her bed. They were with her all the time when they were babies." She frowned. "Of course, the boys were sent to boarding school at seven."

"Seven!" I said.

"Can you imagine little Fergus leaving home in a year and a half?" she asked, visibly shuddering.

"Don't worry," I said, squeezing her hands. "He's not at boarding school yet. You can go home and see him in half an hour."

"It's so hard, Peter, going from being with them every single minute to—this. To being away from them day after day."

"It's what you wanted," I said.

"I know it's what I wanted, and I love it. But you know, there's this little playground on the road behind the theater, and whenever I pass by at lunchtime I see all these little kids running around with their mothers watching them—"

"Or their nannies."

"—and I just miss Fergus and Liam and Jack so much."

"You used to hate going to the playground."

"I hated going to the playground EVERY DAY," she said. "If someone had only told me it wouldn't last forever. That endless drudgery. Scraping potatoes off the floor while someone chucks peas at my hair. One of them always sick—wasn't one of them always sick? The only reward for a day spent in nonstop, exhausted motion was that the kids weren't hungry and the house was only marginally dirtier than it had been at breakfast. That treadmill. I was horrible at it and I'm horribly sorry. And now they're all grown up!"

"They're four and five." I laughed.

"But look," she said. "We've had an entire dinner without interruptions from the kids, and I'm sitting here missing them. When you're in the middle of it you just can't see your way out on the other end, Peter. That's what it is. Now I'm feeling nostalgic. I want those babies back." She smiled slyly and added, "We could always have another one."

"Or we could always just fuck," I said.

While Georgie and I were out that evening, Fergus tore up his handwriting book.

"I can't do it *ploperly*," he said about his lowercase *g*'s, and threw himself on the floor.

Emma was apologetic when we got home, twisting her hands and wincing as if afraid we would blame her for the ruined book. "I was taking something from the oven," she said, "and by the time I turned round to look at him he'd already ripped it in two."

"It's not your fault," Georgie said. "I hate that school."

"He didn't want to talk to me about it at all," Emma said. "But he seemed quite happy later on."

Georgie looked at me with an expression that was both pained and imploring. "You have to find out what's upsetting him," she said. "Talk to him."

"He's a five-year-old boy. He's not going to talk."

"What do you mean he's not going to talk? He never stops talking."

"Not about things that make sense."

"This isn't like him at all. Liam, yes. Jack even—he would see it as a big joke. But Fergus would never destroy a book. He's too serious and obedient. That school is making him feel bad about himself. He already feels like he's behind, and now his mother's abandoned him."

"Relax," I told her. "It's not that big a deal."

The next day was Saturday, and when the boys woke us up early, we decided to take everybody swimming. Fergus had learned to swim over the summer, and there was a quiet confidence that built in him in the pool that I was unable to witness anywhere else in his life. I thought if he were concentrating on swimming he might be his usual loquacious self and I could get some information out of him.

He was slow to get in. He put in his toe and shook his head, then moved closer, as if coaxed by some invisible doppelgänger. He paused, thought about it, waited, and then began to ease himself into the water.

He reminded me so much of myself at that age—which is to say I ached for him. He was the kind of kid I was, always watching to see how everybody else did it before trying it himself. Watching others have fun more than having fun himself. And not really minding so much.

"Are you having some problem at school?" I asked once he had made it into the pool. I sounded like American Dad in an after-school special.

"No," he replied, incredulous at the question. "I love school."

"Why did you rip up your book?" I asked.

He spun around in the water, then dove and splashed me.

"I don't like coyotes," he said when he came up for air. "Coyotes are scary."

He dove again.

"What the hell does that mean?" I said to the underwater boy, suspecting it was his mysterious coded language for "Shut up, Dad."

I shut up and swam with him toward the shallow end, where Georgie was trying to control the twins, who wore water wings and felt indestructible.

Fergus, in constant conversation with his doppelgänger, began to practice his pencil dives.

After he came up again I grabbed him, making him giggle by pretending I was going to throw him across the pool. I held him above me, his thin ribs, his five-year-old torso balancing lightly on my hand. I always thought of him as my big boy, but he was still so slight, so much in need of my protection.

"My boy," I whispered as I brought him down closer to me.

He clung to my neck. "Dad," he said, "some teachers are cruel, right? It's cruel to say, if you're doing your best work, 'That's scribbling,' isn't it?"

Georgie, overhearing, gave me a pained expression and slapped the water with her palm.

Then she needed to yell at Liam for kicking Jack.

The daredevil twins: somewhere in themselves they must believe that if one dies the other will carry on. They have each other, while all Fergus has is his bundle of insecurities.

Georgie went in to speak to Fergus's teacher Monday morning before rehearsal.

"I'm not surprised," Miss Joanne said after she heard Georgie's story. "I would say his attitude toward the pencil has been rather antagonistic."

"He says you won't let him make his old *g* anymore."

"He was making all his letters uppercase. We've actually had to teach him the correct letter formation." The teacher then began to speak about Fergus's *b* and his *g*, pronounced not as *bee* and *gee*, but phonetically, as *buh* and *guh*. She told Georgie, "It helps if you practice his letters with him. Show him the motion of the *buh* and the *guh* and the *eh*. Then he'll begin to get the idea." She sighed. "In some ways it's too late for his printing, but we do have an opportunity with his joined writing."

"Too late? He's only five."

"Yes, but he's a bit behind the other children, you see. The ones who have been with us since three, or even two and three-quarters, haven't had the chance to learn any bad habits."

"Get them while they're young, huh?" Georgie asked.

Surely Miss Joanne chose to ignore the sarcasm. She nodded vigorously. "It does help," she said. "Usually we don't take in any new children at this age, because often we find they're not up to our standard."

"Standard?" asked Georgie. "We're not talking about cars coming off an assembly line." When Miss Joanne made no answer, Georgie said, "Are we?"

"Look," Miss Joanne said, rummaging around on her desk for something else to show Georgie. "It's really all about pencil control. You can see it in his coloring." She held out a sad example for Georgie to see—a page of Fergus's vegetables, shaded so faintly you could barely see the lines of crayon. "Ignoring for a moment that he's done the vegetables in all the wrong colors, you'll see that he has absolutely no respect for the lines."

"But at home he would barely be expected to hold a pencil yet," Georgie said. "He'd still be playing with blocks all day."

"Really," Miss Joanne murmured, so remarkably uninterested that

Georgie burst into tears. In the absence of emotion, Georgie has always felt comfortable supplying it for everyone. Miss Joanne was forced to hand her a tissue.

"I'm sorry," Georgie said. "It's just that they've never known their mother working like this, not every day, not in this all-consuming way. They're used to having me at home, and now we've got this nanny and we live in a new house, a new country. Their lives have just changed so much."

"Oh, the boys have settled in quite quickly," Miss Joanne said kindly. "Children are remarkably resilient, you know. I shouldn't worry about it if I were you."

Usually Georgie hated it when people said children are resilient. To her it seemed that what they really meant was, *By the time they figure out how much we've fucked them up it won't be us paying the therapy bills.* But Miss Joanne's tone was seductively reassuring, and Georgie decided to believe her. The boys did seem fine, wearing their school uniforms, learning how to tie their ties, letting a run in the park after school serve as a substitute for playing their secret spy game in the backyard.

She knew she took her children's problems too much to heart, but she couldn't help herself. Probably no other mother would actually cry over her son's lack of pencil control. Sitting there with Miss Joanne, Georgie missed Fergus so much she felt she was going to pass out. She knew he was just on the other side of the wall and yet the distance felt greater than when she was farther away, in North London at the theater. He was her sweet, sad, old soul, Fergus—she had so wanted to name him after her father and yet sometimes she felt that because of the shared name, her grief for her father enshrouded her small son as well.

When Georgie left Miss Joanne—nothing really resolved—she peeked in Fergus's classroom. He was standing quietly in line with his classmates, ready to go outside for recess. He wasn't giggling or chatting, but he didn't look unhappy, either. As he turned to follow the line outside, she saw his shoulders droop in a pronounced, almost exaggerated way, and it was all she could do to keep from scooping him up and running off with him.

But she had to go—she was already late for rehearsal. Slipping behind the door, she was no more than two feet from Fergus while he and his class walked past. She fought the urge to reach out and smooth his sweet brown curls. She had the absurd premonition that he was walking away from her forever and that if she left to go to the theater she would never see him again.

Finally hurrying to the tube, she felt miserable at leaving him there, all wrong, but she needed to shake that feeling, to push the image of Fergus's drooping shoulders down as far as she could in order to summon what she needed to get back into Mrs. Jordan's world.

They adored me, Miss Williams.

They adored me.

But once I had left Richard Ford for the Duke, they also mocked me. They would not allow an actress a private life, nor did they offer that luxury to a king's son.

How did that dreadful rhyme go? Oh yes:

As Jordan's high and mighty squire
Her playhouse profits designs to skim;
Some folks audaciously inquire
If he keeps her or she keeps him.

The cartoons were deplorable. Oh, Miss Williams, you would not believe what they drew. It was a terribly unfortunate twist of fate that a chamber pot was called a jordan in those days, for they were continually drawing the Duke with a chamber pot on his head. Public Jordan, they said, open to all parties.

You see? Now even I am laughing. They were wickedly clever, these satirists. From my superiority in my profession, I have always had many enemies, but until then they had been confined to people of the same profession. Now the satirists were at work, and as they could find no fault with me as a performer, they caught at every opportunity to injure me as a woman.

I was able to smile at their cleverness until they became very severe, unjustly so, by asserting that I had totally abandoned my three daughters in order to be with the Duke. This was a charge that hurt me extremely; everything else I fairly expected and was prepared for, but my girls were but nine, four, and two years old, and nothing could induce me to loosen those tender ties.

The viciousness raged on, and one day I was taken so ill I was absolutely obliged to miss a few performances at the Haymarket. When I returned to the theatre, playing Roxalana in The Sultan, I was greeted by jeers and hisses. I continued my part, and even when they began shouting at me I refused to quit the stage and instead chose to leave my character for a moment and address the audience directly, like so:

"Ladies and gentlemen, I should conceive myself utterly unworthy of your favour if the slightest ark of public disapprobation did not affect me very sensibly. Since I have had the honour and the happiness to please you, it has been my constant endeavor to merit your approbation.

"Nothing can be more cruel and unfounded than the insinuation that I absented myself from the theatre from any other cause than real inability, from illness, to sustain my part in the entertainment. I believe myself to be under the public protection, and I am accountable to you and resent the insinuation that I do not take my profession seriously.

"If you could drive me from that profession, you would take from me the only income I have, or mean to possess, the whole earnings of which, upon the past, and one-half for the future, I have already settled upon my children."

They listened to me, Miss Williams. The jeers and hisses subsided; my speech had drawn them toward me again, and all was well.

It grew so difficult to bear what the public had to say about my life, and I began to think it might be preferable to disassociate myself from the Duke for the sake of the profession as well as my children. I could not decide what course to take, Miss Williams, but while I was deciding, I felt those first little flutterings—so familiar after the times I had already been a mother, yet always accompanied by a moment of puzzling before the complete recognition—and after that, I knew what I must do about the Duke.

And, the day's rehearsal finished, the writer smiling, the director managing a generous nod, Georgie felt elated, in love with this character, this life she had now, in love with it, and not wanting to leave it behind to go home for the evening.

Our first child, George, ushered in the first month of 1794. It was not an easy birth, but he was in perfect health and I nursed him for five months at home and then kept him at the theatre with me when I returned to the stage.

Sheridan was so relieved to have me back that he gave me a new contract, and made it a generous one. I was now to act, sing, and perform any and every character for five years at thirty guineas a week.

Sheridan wanted me to do Rosalind to start and I said, Do you honestly expect me to squeeze into those breeches? Of course he did! How the audiences have always loved to see me disguised as a boy!

Ah, Rosalind! Such life she breathed into me. I could not do without her.

And the Duke! Such dear enchanting professions of love he gave me. How happy I was, and how I flattered myself that his dear dear love would not abate by time. My heart and happiness were in his power, Miss Williams, and I might with truth add my life, for I felt should he cease to love me I must cease to live.

I decided then I should give up neither the Duke nor the stage.

A year after George's birth, Sophy arrived, and no sooner was I back on stage than the Duke's third child was on his way to join these dear two. We were beginning to run out of room for all of us and the Duke engaged Sir John Soane to design an extra wing at Clarence Lodge. But just then the king made a gracious and unexpected gift. He made the Duke the Ranger of Bushy Park and with the title came the grand estate of Bushy—the house and its one thousand acres of parkland. It was given in the handsomest manner possible; it was given unasked and consequently the greatest favor.

Dear Bushy! Never before in my life had I known such a large, comfortable home. It was a beautiful house, with lovely curving corridors, and rooms enough on the top floor for all the children we had and those that were still to come. The Duke immediately talked of improvements and began by rebuilding the old stables and altering the colonnades. Soane was instructed to put in a bath and a shower.

It was my most fervent wish to make this home agreeable to the Duke, and along with the children, to experience great, very great, happiness there. I installed my three elder daughters with my sister Hester less than a quarter-mile away, and as for the theatre, Drury Lane was just a bit more than two hours by coach.

How can I describe for you the miracle that was Bushy? I can only say I felt like Nell in The Devil to Pay *after the conjurer transforms her from a poor cobbler's wife to a wealthy lady of the manor:*

"What pleasant Dreams I have had To-night! Methought I was in Paradise, upon a Bed of Violets and Roses, and the sweetest Husband by my side. Ha! bless me where am I now? What sweets are these? No Garden in the Spring can equal them; not new blown Roses with the Morning Dew upon them. Am I on a Bed? The sheets are sarsenet sure, no Linen was ever so fine. What a gay silken Robe have I got? Oh Heaven! I dream! Yet if this be a Dream, I would not wish to wake again. Sure I died last Night, and went to Heaven, and this is it."

Bushy became the dearest home I have ever known. Miss Sketchley was there, and she remembers, don't you, Miss Sketchley?

(No thank you, Miss Sketchley, I do not want any more tea. No, nor bread and jam just now. There is a constant gloom hangs over this house and it makes my appetite disappear. Thank you, Miss Sketchley. Thank you. You may go.)

But dear Bushy! The sunlight streamed in, the deer grazed around us, and a baby came nearly every year, exasperating poor Sheridan, who threw his hands up and asked, "Why must they all be born in the middle of the season?"

*L*ess than a week after she spoke to Fergus's teacher, Georgie was an hour into a morning's rehearsal when the school called about Liam. He had thrown up and they wanted her to come collect him.

"He throws up sometimes," she told the school secretary over the phone. "And then he's fine. Can I talk to him?" She was sitting cross-legged on the stage next to the contents of her bag, which she had dumped out to find the ringing phone.

No, they said, she couldn't talk to him. He was lying down. He was unwell. Unwell children must be collected.

"Okay," Georgie said, and then to Piers and Nicola, "Sorry, guys. My son's sick and I have to go."

"Isn't there someone else?" Nicola asked. "A nanny of some sort? We can't afford to lose a day's rehearsal for this kind of thing."

Georgie took a deep breath. "Give me a minute," she said. She took her phone into the lobby of the theater so she wouldn't have Piers and Nicola as audience.

She tried Emma, but Emma took a course in the mornings and had her phone switched off. Then she tried Jean, the neighbor with whom she'd done little more than exchange phone numbers. There was no answer at Jean's house, and Georgie didn't have her mobile number, so she called me.

"I can't," I told her. "I'm sorry. I'm just going into this meeting."

"It's an emergency, Peter. They're shooting daggers at me. They really don't want to hear about my sick kid. And the school's so inflexible. 'Sick children must be collected!'" she mimicked.

"You can't blame them, Georgie. I'm sorry," I said. "It's not something I can get out of. Can't you get Emma?"

"I can't reach her. She's got her phone off. Peter, please."

"Look, they're sitting there in the conference room waiting for me. I've got to go in. Now."

"How many times did I take care of them while they were sick and you went off to work?"

"I'm not going to play that game, Georgie," I said.

"The one time I've got something. It's so unfair. Nothing's changed. It's always me." She hung up before I could say something I would regret: *Whose job got us over here? Whose job's paying the bills?*

Her stomach in knots, she had no choice but to ignore Piers and Nicola's disapproval. She rushed off to the school, but even in a taxi it was a full thirty minutes before she got there.

"Oh, sweetheart," she said when she saw Liam. He was sitting on the black leather couch in the entrance hall, wearing a too-small shirt that wasn't his own, holding his throw-up clothes in a plastic bag on his lap.

Georgie rushed in with a mother's reflex, the cool back of the hand against his forehead. "You're not warm," she said. "How do you feel?"

"I guess fine," he said. "I don't know. Maybe a little fine and a little not fine."

"He was much happier when he heard Mummy was on her way, weren't you, Liam?" asked the secretary, smiling.

"What made you sick?" Georgie asked.

"T-Bone," he said.

"What?"

"T-Bone from Year One," Liam said.

"You have a kid in your school called T-Bone?" Georgie asked.

"Thibaud," corrected the secretary. "He's French."

"Oh," Georgie said.

She turned back to Liam. "How did he make you sick?" she asked.

"He said I couldn't play football in the garden with the big boys."

"Hmm." Georgie looked at the secretary, but she had returned to her typing. Georgie stood up and approached her. "Do you know what happened?"

The secretary shook her head. "Miss Arabella just sent him down here."

"Could I just go up and talk to her for a minute?"

"She's on lunchroom duty at the moment."

"Okay." Georgie decided to get more information from Liam first. She knelt down in front of him and took his hand.

"Liam," she said, "how did Thibaud not letting you play football make you sick?"

"I don't know if I can explain this," Liam said. "Will you believe me? I—"

"Of course I'll believe you. I'm your mother who loves you."

"Well, okay, but it's like he has magical powers. No, really, Mom, very more powerfuler powers than me or anybody in the whole school. I just asked can I play football and he said no, only good players can play."

"You're a good player," Georgie said.

Liam nodded. "I told him that but he said no and Alfie and Nicholas said I can't play and they all said I was rubbish at football, but Mom, I'm not rubbish at football." Here Liam began to cry and Georgie pulled him onto her lap. He buried his face in her neck, her little tough-guy twin, the one who was usually terrorizing his brother but now needed his mom.

"All right, sweetie, we'd better get you home," Georgie said. "But let me go talk to Miss Arabella first. It sounds like those boys were being mean to you."

"Alfred was cheering for T-Bone and Nicholas was cheering for T-Bone and all I heard was only a little fly cheering for me."

"Oh, Liam." Georgie said, hugging him.

"That was when he used his most magicalest powers to make me throw up."

Georgie gently nudged him off her lap. The secretary nodded when Georgie asked if she could leave Liam there for a minute more.

In the lunchroom, at least a hundred boys and girls sat with trays of chicken curry and a side plate of fruit. The amazing thing about the room, though, was its silence. Georgie was almost reluctant to say "Excuse me," and as soon as she did speak, every pair of eyes in the room was on her. Miss Arabella joined her in the hallway just outside the lunchroom.

"How's Liam?" Miss Arabella asked.

"He's okay," Georgie said. "Better, I think. I don't think he's sick, but he seems to be upset by some boys who wouldn't let him play with them. I think that's what made him sick."

Miss Arabella nodded. "I thought it might be something like that."

"You did? Why?"

"He's had a little bit of trouble finding his place, Liam has. Nothing to be alarmed about. I would say he's made some nice friends, but he's not quite sure where he stands."

"Oh," Georgie said, feeling the force of a blow. Her little boy didn't know where he stood. "Oh. There's this one boy, Thibaud, he mentioned in particular."

Miss Arabella made a face. "Ah," she said. "I shall have a word with his teacher." Her manner was so reassuring that Georgie instantly felt comforted.

"Thank you," she said, and went to take Liam home.

He had her all to himself the rest of the day and she did exactly what he wanted to do. She played dinosaurs with him on the floor of his bedroom, she made him rice cakes and peanut butter, she let him watch his favorite movie all the way through, twice, sitting on her lap. They drew pictures together and danced to silly songs. They did his train puzzle. These were the things she had spent the past five years doing, but with Fergus and Jack gone there were no fights, no tears, no whining. She could be a world-class mother, she decided, given one child at a time.

But, "Can't you stay with me?" Liam asked when Emma arrived home with Jack and Fergus after the school day ended.

"I've got to meet with my dialect coach tonight," Georgie said. "He's the one who helps Mommy with her different voices for the play."

"You NEVER put me to bed," Liam wailed. He began to push at her with his two hands. "Emma ALWAYS puts me to bed," he yelled, and this was the beginning of a tantrum that did not abate until after she was out the door. The closeness of the afternoon, her penance, was all wiped away by the screams she could hear almost to the end of the street.

She fought the tears. Liam would be mad at her until morning. How could she possibly leave him in that state?

How did Mrs. Jordan do it, Georgie wanted to know. With *thirteen* children? How could she live the life of her family and of the stage all at once?

During our first ten years at Bushy, seven more children were born to join the three I had already given the Duke: first Mary, then Frederick (dear Freddles!), Elizabeth, Adolphus, called Lolly, Augusta, always called Ta, Augustus, called Tuss, and finally Amelia, my dear little Mely. We named them all after the Duke's brothers and sisters, the royal dukes and princesses.

How those children thrived at Bushy, riding their ponies, chasing dogs, coursing for hares, fishing in the Thames. They were in fresh air all the time. It was an enviable existence, and one that I could scarcely compare to my own impoverished childhood in Dublin.

When we were at Bushy the house overflowed from every part, my young family playing about us. Of course I was always leaving them all for Drury Lane or the provinces.

"Children, Mama must go to the theatre now. Let us have a kiss before I go. No, Sophy, don't be cross. I will bring you a very pretty work box and my dear George a writing case and Henry a new-fashioned lantern."

I had a fine writing case in my own carriage, and began writing to the Duke and the children nearly as soon as I left home. I wrote to the Duke every day, you see, and he to me:

I wish I was at home. When I am here I feel like a person deserted by the whole world, and open to all kind of unpleasant situations. God bless you and the dear dear children. No applause or success can for a moment compensate for the loss of your society and the happiness of being with the dear babes.

Kiss the dear little ones. I dream of the baby all night, dear little fellow. I have sworn I felt him in bed several times.

My love and blessing to all,
Your dear Dora.
Your dearest Mama.

I'm going to quit," Georgie said.

"Quit what?" I asked.

"The play."

"Nonsense," I said.

"They need me," she said. "The boys. They're acting up. Things are falling apart. I can't stand how guilty I feel when I'm at work and how tired I am when I'm at home."

"They're doing fine," I said.

But the leaving and returning made her miss them so terribly. Her eyes ate them up when they came into view.

Suddenly she seemed to be ending up in tears at every rehearsal. She began to hate Nicola, whose let-me-show-you-how-it's-done attitude made her bristly and defensive. And Piers, who was so silent, with that bemused know-it-all look on his face, infuriated her with those damned notes. She craved less direction, not more. She needed to attune herself to Mrs. Jordan in her own way, to shed her home life when she entered the theater and take on this woman as her own second skin.

"What's with Piers and Nicola, anyway?" Georgie asked Graham when she met him for coffee one morning before rehearsal. "I don't think she likes me at all, and I couldn't begin to tell you what he thinks."

"I don't think Nicola likes anybody," Graham answered, "except for Piers, whom she worships, by the way. I know Nicola quite well, really, as well as anybody. I've worked with her since just after university. She'll tell you that theater is not hierarchical, that each new production creates a family with a new child, but she'll be a right old witch while she's doing it."

"Great," Georgie said.

"Don't let her give you shit."

"That's the thing," Georgie said. "She's polite, she's respectful. She's very, very good at what she does. She's not giving me shit. Still, I have this vague sense that shit is being given."

"How very English of you, Georgie," Graham said. "Never underestimate the lethalism of the passive voice."

"I can't seem to make any headway with them. If it was one or the other, maybe I'd have a chance, but with both of them . . . She's so . . ."

"Steely and pedantic?"

"And he's so . . ."

"Sexy and inscrutable?"

Georgie snorted. "Are they, like, a couple?"

Graham shrugged. "Probably? But you should watch yourself anyway, Georgie. Piers has quite a reputation."

"Please," Georgie said. "I'm a big girl."

"Uh-huh," Graham said, nodding wisely. "Don't forget I was there during your freakish backstage episodes with—"

"Shut up!"

"What was his name?"

"Shut up."

"That squalid production of *Othello*, wasn't it?"

"Shut *up*." She pounded on his arm. "That was years ago."

"And you're still embarrassed about it, aren't you?"

"Excruciatingly so. But that was before I was married."

"My dear, this is the theater." Graham smiled and stood up to go. "Look, Georgie," he said. "You've been terribly lucky with this part, don't forget that. Quit your whingeing, and please remember to thank me in the process. Nicola and Piers adore you. I hear fantastic things from them. If the notices are good they'll do their best to move the show to the West End."

"That's great," Georgie said, "You're great, Graham. I wish I could just sit around and talk with *them* like this."

"Oh, for God's sake, Georgie, you're such a child in so many ways. If you want to talk to them, just invite them out for a drink."

"Do you think?"

"Yes, I do," Graham said paternally. He looked at his watch. "Now don't be late for rehearsal. I'm not promising they'll listen to you, but it's worth a try."

*U*sually when Georgie became stuck in a play, it was the text that got her through—she would return to the character's words and find a way to bring them to life. But this time it seemed there was something wrong with the words themselves. There was something off with the character, so much so that the final scenes of the play felt completely false. If she held on to her own view of Mrs. Jordan as a woman whose life depended on the theater, there was no way she could accept the play's ending, where Mrs. Jordan died calling out for her children. All traces of her life as an actress or as a lover were gone by the end of the play; she was left lonely, desolate, bereft of everything but the hope of seeing her children. To Georgie, this was all wrong. She took Graham's advice and invited Nicola and Piers out for a drink after rehearsal one night. She had scouted out the neighborhood and found among several loud pubs a wine bar, dark and smoky as a pub but quieter—no TV, no football match on, not much of an after-work crowd.

They walked quietly from the theater, Piers in his jean jacket, Nicola in her brown wool blazer, Georgie with her agenda. So much of her time at rehearsal was spent with the two of them side by side, looking at her, so once they were in the wine bar she positioned herself next to Piers, hoping he would prove to be an ally, with Nicola across the table.

Georgie rarely drank, but she ordered a glass of wine anyway. Merlot sounded authoritative and strong, so she asked for that, but Piers and Nicola both ordered sauvignon blanc, and Georgie felt she had lost the upper hand even before she had it. She sighed, and waited for the wine to arrive before she began.

"Okay, you guys," she said. "This is what I think. I don't think she should die at the end."

Piers said nothing, but smiled a little too condescendingly. Nicola said, "Oh?" and mildly raised an eyebrow.

"I mean, of course she dies at the end, everyone dies at the end, but we don't have to show it. She died because she wasn't acting anymore. If we end with one of her greatest roles, one of her most famous speeches, it allows her to reclaim her life." She heard her pitch rise with insistence and tried to quiet it. She wanted to play this calmly. She took it down a notch. "The life of the stage, I mean."

"She died missing her children," Piers said slowly, evenly.

"Of course, but she missed the stage equally," Georgie said. She shifted slightly sideways to look at him, her knee knocking into the top of his thigh. "It was her life's work. She loved her children, but she needed the stage."

"She didn't have a choice with either of those things," Nicola said. "If she had had a choice, would she have had thirteen children? And acting was the only career open to women at the time."

"You can't say she didn't have a choice," she told Nicola, "that her career and her children were both by default."

"She certainly rose to the occasion on both counts," Nicola said.

"She was a doting mother. And she was lucky. She happened to be the greatest comic actress of her time."

"She didn't *happen to be*," Georgie said. "It's who she was. She may have died asking for her children, but she also died asking for applause."

"Ah, but that is just your interpretation, Georgie," Piers said, and Georgie turned to glare at him, hating him for that "just." "So much of the play is taken from her correspondence," he continued. "She left hundreds of letters, you know. Her feelings at the end are expressed unequivocally."

"I know the words," Georgie said. *It is not, believe me, the feelings of pride, avarice, or the absence of those comforts I have all my life been accustomed to, that is killing me by inches; it is the loss of my only remaining comfort, the hope I used to live on from time to time of seeing my children*—the very last lines of the play.

"They're powerful words," Piers said. "And they're her own. Lifted directly from her letters."

"But that's not the whole story," Georgie interrupted. "She also said that acting kept her alive. And it's less than a year after she retires that she dies." *Like my dad,* she didn't add. Fergus Connolly had died of a heart attack a mere seven months after he officially turned his construction business over to Georgie's brothers. In many ways Georgie had never recovered from the loss of her father, and she knew she would always link his death with his giving up his life's work.

She fought her way back from his memory to the table.

"What you have to realize, Georgie," Nicola was saying, "is that Mrs. Jordan was an entirely self-invented woman. Her name, her accent, *everything*, was made up."

"What do you mean by that, exactly?" Georgie picked up her glass and tipped it so that the wine touched her lips, though she didn't take a drink.

"I mean she was a master at playing. At putting on. Even her letters are at times contrived. We don't know much about what she really felt."

"I disagree, Nicola," Piers said. "She was, for all her complications, a very forthright woman. I don't know if I would use the word 'simple,' but—"

"Simple, Piers?" Nicola said. "Oh, come on."

"Pure?" he said, smiling. "Is that better?"

"What's coming across to me, Georgie," Nicola said, letting the flirtatious smile she had used with Piers turn businesslike for Georgie, "is that you're arguing for the actress, and Piers and I are arguing for the woman."

Piers nodded at Nicola. "Dora's first biographer, her close friend James Boaden, insisted it was the breakup with the Duke in 1811 that caused her eventual destruction. It ruined her health, it ruined her spirit. She never got over it. I believe his words were, 'The woman in her was too powerful for the genius.'"

"That's very condescending," Georgie said. "Also chauvinistic."

"I don't necessarily think that's how it's meant."

"I do," Georgie said. "I necessarily do. No one would say it about a man."

"Come on, Georgie," Piers said. "If a man goes to war, he dies as a soldier but he also dies as a man. We're not taking about sexism. We're talking about humanity."

Damn you both, Georgie wanted to say. Would have said if she knew them better. She was completely exasperated. Nicola was sure her interpretation was the right one, Piers viewed himself as the expert, but Georgie could see Mrs. Jordan only as a modern, working woman struggling with the demands of career, motherhood, and love affair, trying to do the right thing on all fronts, failing often and miserably everywhere, occasionally meeting the great and thrilling successes that made it all worth it. Georgie refused to question her own impulses about this character, this woman who loved her family but lived for the stage. How could she, when Mrs. Jordan's struggle was also exactly her own?

"Damn you," she did say aloud, but gently, getting up to leave, her wine untouched.

Outside, the war waged on, but I cut my path straight between Bushy and the theatre. I tried to stay out of politics; my world remained populated by my characters and my children.

The years began to grow a bit heavy on the Duke and me. It was never the Duke's fault in any shape that I made those excursions to the theatre, but I began to see more clearly the injustice I did to him, he always with the children at Bushy and I always departing or returning from London or the provinces. After some years, the Duke asked me to be nothing more than the mistress of Bushy, and in that I felt I must oblige.

When it was known I was to retire at the Duke's beckoning, the Morning Herald *ran an epitaph:*

Sacred to the Memory
of
Mrs Dorothy Jordan,
Late of Drury Lane Theatre,

poor, injured mortality,
snatched
from the fostering embrace of
Public Admiration
In the full vigour of her attraction
That raised it.

Then it was I who stayed at Bushy with the children while the Duke was away from Mondays to Saturdays. The Duke so desired a naval command that he ventured weekly to Portsmouth or Southampton simply to be near the sea, and to plead his case for a posting in the navy. The wish nearest his heart was to serve as marine minister, but neither the king nor any of the ministers would help him secure such a posting.

He continued to direct his improvements to Bushy from whatever corner of England he found himself in. How he loved to move rooms and fill in windows, put up walls where there were none—and take down those that were already there. He was forever altering my bedroom just when I was in the family way, and I often found myself wishing the room were done or he was at Bushy. Honestly, I didn't know how on earth to manage the bricklayers!

You may suppose the life I led with the children at Bushy after my retirement, Miss Williams. Such reports I sent along to the Duke:

"Ah yes, the doctor has advised postponing inoculating little Tuss until the weather is decidedly cooler. Poor dear, I must wean him tomorrow. The rest of the young ones are well, though Lolly's cold is rather troublesome.

"Sophy has come in very cross, I'm afraid, and complains of a headache. I fear her constitution will shortly undergo a change. It is with the *greatest difficulty that I can get her to stir out of her bedroom or hit on anything to amuse her.*

"Freddles's new boots are really very excellent ones!"

I was glad, for the Duke's sake, that he was often away. At least he had a relief from the constant scenes of distress among the children, which, I must tell you, Miss Williams, were very nearly too much for me.

I don't get it," Georgie said. "Why did she retire?"

"He asked her to. He was a man, and he was royalty," Piers said. "In Regency England those were two very good reasons."

"But she's miserable. She can't stand it at home." Georgie frowned. "'Freddles's new boots are really very excellent ones!'" she mimicked. "She's dying, she's going nuts."

"You're capturing it perfectly," Piers said.

"Believe me, I've been there," Georgie said. "Two hundred years later and it's exactly the same thing. You want to spend every single moment with your children and still have a fulfilling life at work."

Georgie and Piers had spent the entire afternoon rehearsing the Bushy scenes. With less than three weeks to go to the play's opening Nicola had to miss a day and a half of rehearsal, so Piers had taken over. Unorthodox, and perhaps a measure of how much Nicola worshipped Piers that she had let him in on her directorial role, but Nicola didn't want Georgie to fall behind.

"Absolutely perfect," he said. "So perfect that I suggest we play truant tomorrow and do a little period research."

"Such as?" Georgie asked.

"There's a portrait at Kenwood House you really must see," Piers said. "Mrs. Jordan as Viola. Kenwood House. Have you been?"

"No. I keep meaning to, but—"

"Oh, it's a lovely spot. At the top of Hampstead Heath. Why don't I meet you there tomorrow midday and we can have a look together?" His gaze was steady, and he smiled at her with such warmth that she felt for a minute as if they were friends and it was the most natural thing in the world for him to invite her somewhere.

"Sure," she said slowly. "Why not?"

Up until now Piers had been distantly cordial, Georgie respectful and a little shy. This overture of his—was it to be their first date? Surely she wasn't thinking of it that way or she would never have told me about it, with a grimace and roll of the eyes: "He wants me to see this *picture*."

She readied herself as for a date, wearing lipstick, brushing her long hair vigorously and leaving it down, dressing in a brown suede skirt and plum-colored blouse, tall suede boots that showed off her shapely calves and ended just under her lovely round knees.

Kenwood House was a white stately home full of paintings by Dutch masters and English portrait artists. It was in such a rural part of London that Georgie felt she was in the country. They walked down a gravelly path to the house and walked through quietly, looking at all the rooms until they found the painting Piers wanted Georgie to see. It was small, not really remarkable, just a portrait of Mrs. Jordan dressed as Viola disguised as a boy. Georgie preferred the full-length portraits she had seen in other places—the artists' depiction of the whole woman helped Georgie to relate to Mrs. Jordan physically. This was just a pretty picture, and she told Piers so.

"Yes, but it's one of her most famous roles," he countered. "I think it's important for you to see it."

"I think you just didn't want to do any work today," she teased, "and you didn't want to get in trouble with Nicola."

When he didn't deny it they both started to laugh.

"Come," he said, "let's go waste more time."

They left the house and wandered the grounds, walking down a small path that headed down toward the pond. It was early afternoon, but the mid-December days were getting so short it already felt halfway to night. Georgie closed her eyes and tried to pretend she was at Bushy. The houses were roughly the same age, and similar in style. Georgie had tried to visit Bushy, which still stood near Hampton Court Palace in the south of London, but it was used as some sort of scientific research facility now and was closed to the public. Even her New York persistence hadn't gained her entrance to the house, and she had let it drop after a couple of tries, deciding she didn't want to see Mrs. Jordan's beloved Bushy full of desks and computers, anyway.

They ended the day with a coffee together in the Kenwood House tea shop. It was the first time Georgie had ever sat face-to-face with Piers—alone—and as she nervously fiddled with the cutlery on the table she realized she felt as vulnerable as she did when onstage rehearsing for him, trying to get it right. *For him*: she had never before worked on a play where the writer was so present. She felt an irrefutable blurring of creator and creation, and an insanely powerful need to please.

"How did you get interested in Mrs. Jordan, anyway?" she decided to ask him.

He smiled and stirred his coffee, though he had not put milk or sugar into it. "You might say for sentimental reasons. I'm distantly related to her, you know."

"No, I didn't know. How would I have known? Could it be you didn't tell me?" She smiled, teasing him. Was she smiling too much? She felt she was smiling too much.

"On my mother's side. When we were high-tempered or theatrical as kids she'd always say, 'Oh, that's the Mrs. Jordan coming out in you.' I never really understood that Mrs. Jordan was a real person. I thought my mother had made her up. 'That's the Mrs. Jordan in you.' I thought it was an expression, along the lines of 'The devil made me do it.' Or 'The cat's got your tongue.'"

"Or 'It's just the drink talking,'" Georgie said. Always one of her father's favorite sayings.

"Exactly. It wasn't a family connection anyone was actually proud of. Being a king's bastard great-great-great-great-grandnephew is not exactly something one dines out on. It wasn't until I was doing my A-levels in history that I came across a reference to Dora Jordan and discovered she was a real person. And it was much later before I was old enough to appreciate that she wasn't just some gold-digging bimbo. I've worked out she was probably the best thing that ever happened to old William. He was a playboy, a wastrel, and none too bright to begin with. She had by far the nobler character. Kind, warmhearted, very generous. She worked like a dog, earning money to support him, but I believe she genuinely loved him, don't you?"

"I do," Georgie said, stupidly flattered that he was asking her opinion.

"I know what it looked like from the outside—he cast her off when she grew old and fat and lost that reproductive look—"

"'That reproductive look'?" Georgie asked sharply.

Piers flashed her a smile. "Sorry. I mean to say, things always look sordid and cliché-ridden from the outside, but that's rarely how they are when you get to the heart of the matter. It's never anything so simple as a man walking out on a woman. There's more to it than that, and I wanted to find the real story." He placed his hand on top of Georgie's and said earnestly, "I wanted to tell the truth of her life."

She stared at his hand on hers. It almost seemed more of a transgression to remove it than to leave it there. She had never been this physically close to him before, and she indulged a surge of desire. Pleasurable, controllable. What harm was there in this? She didn't pull her hand away.

She cleared her throat. "I guess you could say all he was doing was starfucking while she was, I don't know, *crownfucking*—"

"That would have been the easy way to look at it, but would it have lasted twenty years? Everything suggests they had a very happy home, great affection for each other and their children. I felt this keen desire to ensoul their romance."

"Which you did," she said.

"Did I? I had hoped to, Georgie, but I'm not so sure I succeeded." Georgie realized she was blushing at his speaking her name, the way she might have felt in high school finding out a boy she liked actually knew who she was. *I have got to stop this,* she was thinking. *I am acting like an idiot.*

Piers continued. "My greatest challenge with the play was that while I had her letters to him, hundreds of them, there is not a single letter extant from him to her. She felt compelled to return them to the Duke's lawyers and advisors after he left her, and they were probably all destroyed. It was maddening to not know with absolute certainty whether he loved her, why he left her, what he felt afterward about what he had done."

"Doesn't the fact that he saved all her letters tell you he must have loved her?"

Piers smiled and nodded. "That's my conclusion, but at the end of the day one is left only with one's best guesses."

"One is," Georgie said, smiling.

Piers finally moved his hand away from hers just as casually as he had put it there.

Was he already trying to seduce her? He had arranged this little outing, a safe daytime meeting on National Trust property, perhaps his first gentle move toward that end. And yet, when I think about that day, when I fill in the scene, I'm not so sure. It could have gone either way, I think, and I'm perhaps more jealous of their talk about the play than of his hand briefly resting on hers. *I am a writer too*, I want to say, inserting myself into that darkening December afternoon at Kenwood House. *Georgie, you could have talked to me about those things.*

"What a process it is," Georgie said. "Here's this woman who lived two hundred years ago, and you had to discover who she was to write the play and now I have to discover who she is all over again so that I can act the part."

"Well, yes. That's the theater, after all."

"No," Georgie said. "I'm talking about something else. What I mean is, everything is re-creation. Nothing is real. It's all . . ." She was unable to articulate it to him and fell quiet again.

"Are you saying there's no truth, only versions?"

"Not at all," she said. "Her life had a truth. It's only you and I who have versions of it."

"Very sweet of you, Georgie. Very pure. But there are dozens of ways of looking at a life. She was a complex woman. Did she love the Duke, did she not love the Duke? Did she miss her children as much as she said she did? It's all a matter of interpretation."

"Exactly," Georgie said. "Yours and mine. But she knew who she was."

"Not according to Nicola," Piers said.

"Nicola's wrong, obviously," Georgie said. "I mean, I know you have to commit to some overriding view of her life. If you're going to write about her, if I'm going to play her, we need our versions to cling to. But underneath it all there's the real Dora Jordan none of us knows."

Piers nodded. "I think anyone trying to write someone's life has to admit that fact at some point in the process. Unless you possess a great deal of blind arrogance, of course. But I do believe if you can get to the central conflict—"

"The main motivation of her life—" Georgie interrupted again.

"—then you've done the life justice," Piers finished. "That's all we're after, we writers."

"But don't you wish you could just go back?" Georgie asked, becoming excited. "Go back and talk to her and just ask her all those things?"

"More than anything," Piers said.

For no real reason Georgie began to laugh.

"What is it?" he asked.

"Nothing," she said. "I don't know." But she was still laughing and he persisted.

"What?"

"It's just that, I don't know, you've suddenly become a three-dimensional character to me."

"A fortunate thing for a playwright, I should say."

"Oh, no," Georgie said. "Playwrights are allowed to be two-dimensional. Most of the ones I've known have been."

"How very kind you are."

"No, really. It's something about the process. Characters require an actor to bring them to life, and it's almost the same thing with playwrights."

"That wouldn't be you, would it?" Piers asked, and the teasing irony of his voice was at odds with the look in his eyes. She smiled shyly and looked down at the hand he had placed on hers just minutes before.

"Well," she said quietly, after a moment, "I've got to be going home now." *Home to my husband. Home to my life.* She had indulged in this fantasy for a moment or two; now it was time to let it go.

"Are you sure?" he asked.

"I'm sure," she said, standing up. Piers got to his feet as well. He took her arm and led her outside. The sky had finished its journey to darkness for that afternoon, and though she disavowed it, he had begun his intrusion into her heart.

I was two full seasons out of the theatre—two full seasons the mistress of Bushy—and then I gave birth to Mely, my tenth child with the Duke. It went as well as could be expected, the old answer in all parts of the world on those occasions. Five boys and five girls I had given the Duke, and when Mely was six months old I convinced the Duke to let me return to Drury Lane.

Why, you ask, Miss Williams? If only the answer were an easy one I would find it less troublesome to satisfy your curiosity.

Fanny and Dodee were now of marrying age, you see, and each required a dowry of ten thousand pounds. Meanwhile, the Duke had failed to secure a naval posting but nonetheless continued to require money for his improvements to Bushy.

And yet money did not serve as the only reason for my return to the stage. Throughout my two years of retirement no one had forgotten me. John Barrister persisted in sending me tragedies, but I told him, notwithstanding there was much pretty writing in the parts, I did not think that I could do myself or the authors any service by undertaking tragedy anymore. I found laughing agreed with me better than crying.

Yes, Miss Williams, I did allow myself to be coaxed back by comedy. ·

Sheridan dropped my wages to thirty pounds per week when I returned. I had grown so large that they spoke of me almost accusingly as plump, matronly, stout, as if I could be anything else after thirteen children.

I was forty-five years old, still playing Rosalind and Viola in breeches. I refused to play Mrs Malaprop or old women in farces. I simply could not bear that.

The audiences still came to see me, Miss Williams; the admirers returned.

Hazlitt said my voice was like the luscious juice of the ripe grape. Thankfully he spoke of my voice and not my form!

Charles Lamb said I was a privileged being, sent to teach mankind what it most wants, joyousness. Shakespeare's woman, he called me, because my Rosalind has been beloved by all of England for these nearly twenty years.

I piqued myself on all this flattery, and to say that I was devoid of talent as an actress would only be begging a compliment. Yet to be plain, Miss Williams, I frequently asked myself as the encore was reiterated, what in the name of reason could call forth such popular enthusiasm? There were many players younger than I, more shapely than I, less troubled in mind than I was or could ever hope to be.

In answer, I may only say that I played each part naturally, that is all. I preferred to read my lines in a way as to show off the character rather than the poet. I knew I had no more than the words I uttered, and yet when I mastered the language of a part, I said to Dame Nature, "My head, hands, feet, and every member about me, are at your commandment."

It is not I but She these audiences are to thank for my return to the stage, and for my performances.

The outing to Kenwood had given Georgie a boost, some new window into Mrs. Jordan, but as soon as Nicola was back she felt her confidence begin to ebb again.

She still couldn't get the last scene right.

The last scene.

The death scene.

There was no way around it. Whether she threw herself into the chaise longue or sank into a chair or let herself sway desperately at the center of the stage, it was a death scene. There could be nothing redemptive until the curtain call.

She couldn't feel Dora's death because Dora did not feel dead to her. After a while it became clear that she was going to have to go to France, where Dora died.

"Imagine that," she told me, "saying, 'I need to go to France,' and then just being able to go."

We couldn't fly back to the States for Christmas because Georgie only had a week off from rehearsals, and the play was scheduled to open the second week in January. More than that, she was worried about losing momentum—taking herself out of her part for a week might be dangerous. So we spent Christmas on our own in London and left on Boxing Day to spend a few days in Paris.

Georgie bought the boys matching blue duffel coats and posed them as gargoyles in front of Notre Dame, hoping for a good photo to send with the belated Christmas cards. We lined up at the Louvre to see the *Mona Lisa*, took a boat trip down the Seine, let the boys run around the Tuileries each afternoon to blow off steam when the day's sightseeing was done.

And then it was time to go to St. Cloud. *San Clu*, it was pronounced, as I learned when I tried to buy train tickets, convinced that repeating *Saint Cloud* in the loud, nasal way you would say it in Minnesota would make it clear to the French ticket agent where I wanted to go.

Georgie had no way of knowing what St. Cloud had been like in 1816, when Dora Jordan was there, but now it was nothing more than an upscale suburb of Paris, flowery and quiet, with hilly streets and a good view of the Eiffel Tower. Unlike many old towns in Europe, where you could imagine simply taking down a few modern signs and having the old town back again, St. Cloud had modernized very efficiently, its new architecture and hip graphics making it impossible to detect any sign of the life Mrs. Jordan might have lived there. The house where she died had been bulldozed decades ago. Even her grave had been moved.

We walked on a gray blustery morning out the long, straight avenue from the train station toward the town's newer cemetery. According to Fergus, each house we passed was more and more like Madeline's. Georgie bought some yellow flowers at a florist's we passed on the way.

When we reached the cemetery, there was a sign on the lodge saying that the *gardien* would not return for an hour.

"It's a small cemetery," Georgie said. "Let's split up and search for Dora's stone."

"Except three-fifths of us can't read," I said.

"They can try," Georgie said. "How hard could it be?" She turned to the boys and told them what to look for. She wrote *Jordan* on a scrap of paper, which they then fought over like a cereal box prize, so she had to write it down twice more.

"What if some of the dead people are ghost-es?" Jack asked.

"There's no such thing," Georgie told him.

Fergus laid a hand on Georgie's arm and said solemnly, "We're going to find Mrs. Jordan, Mommy. If it's the last thing we do, we're going to find Mrs. Jordan."

Georgie threw her arms around him, so in love with her son at that moment.

We lost the boys many times while we searched. It was amazing how quickly all three could disappear, really disappear, behind rows of gravestones, and then materialize again in the midst of some argument with each other.

Jack ran up and clung to me. "Daddy, I'm not going with Liam. Liam always bes a ghost. He keeps saying *whoooo* to me."

"You said *whoooo* to me first," Liam said.

"No, you," said Jack.

"No, you," said Liam.

"*Whoooo*," I said, sending both of them off with shrieks of half-scared giggles.

Georgie and I walked endlessly among the gravestones with her bouquet of flowers. It seemed as if we had read every marker two or three times, and yet after an hour we still had not found Dora's grave.

When the *gardien* returned, Georgie said, "Dora Jordan," to him with what she hoped was a French accent, and after a long string of French he said, in English, "Yes, I know where she is."

She followed him eagerly to the grave, clearly the oldest stone in this modern, symmetrical cemetery. It was surprising that we could have missed it: *Dora Jordan, La plus grande interprète anglaise de la comédie.*

Georgie stood in front of the stone for a few minutes, frowning, trying to decipher the long French inscription on the plaque. She placed the yellow flowers on the grave, and I asked her if she wanted a picture, but she shook her head. When she turned to me I could see the swollen, glassy semicircle of tears under her eyes. I put my arms around her and she nestled her face into my neck.

"I just miss her so much," she said, and then began to laugh. "God, that sounds ridiculous."

We went to a crêperie across the street and bought some peace and quiet by allowing the boys to dump as much powdered sugar as they wanted on their enormous lemony crêpes. Georgie and I ordered savory crêpes and a bottle of wine. She cheered up, but was quiet.

"Any ideas?" I asked her after some time had passed. I tried in my tentative husbandly way to show I was interested in what she thought but didn't want to invade her creative process.

"I'm not sure," she said. "I don't know yet." She was not satisfied, I could see, and not particularly happy with the outing, but she wasn't telling me why.

Later, as we rode the train back into Paris, she stared out the window, holding a sleeping Liam in her lap, cuddling him as if he were still a baby.

It was perhaps the first time she realized how tremendously much time had passed, how long gone Mrs. Jordan really was. This was a place for a dead woman, while the Mrs. Jordan she needed to locate was spectacularly alive.

*O*pening night.

    First night, they call it in London.

In New York, there would have been all our friends, Georgie's mother, her brothers and their wives, a crowd along to celebrate. But after barely four months in London, we still knew almost no one, and Georgie was cautious; she didn't want me to invite my new acquaintances from work, or any of the neighbors she hardly knew. Jean from across the street had been very friendly but Georgie hadn't pursued it, and then one day Jean had shown up at our door with a couple of electrical transformers and said that her husband had suddenly been transferred back to New York.

Every seat was filled—the producers had made sure of that—and in such an intimate theater, those in the front row were practically on the proscenium. I sat with Graham near the back because Georgie was more concerned about our view of the audience than of her.

She came onstage in a lightly powdered wig, fashionable for the times, a yellow silk dress, and though she was meant to be fifty-four years old as the play began, heavy and ill and wracked with despair, they had used no aging makeup on her. She was able to convey what she needed to through her facial gestures, her posture, the slightly breathless delivery that suggested how difficult she found it to speak.

Instantly I was taken back to the night she had first encountered Mrs. Jordan, in her white tank top and jeans, performing in our tiny sitting room only for me.

As she began to trace Mrs. Jordan's life back to her youth, a mesmerizing vigor entered her movements; her posture and her breathing altered, the syllables lengthening or shortening as she moved from poor illegitimate Irish girl to famous London actress, mistress of a royal duke, to mother of thirteen children. And she was Rosalind, Viola, Helena, the poor girl from *The Fair Penitent*, someone called Lady Teazle in a part that lasted only a moment but that had the audience roaring before she miraculously exchanged humor for pathos in the next scene.

The mere addition of a feathered hat and pointed boots or the adjustment of a wig changed everything about her, so subtly that you noticed nothing but the complete transformation.

She was good, so good at this, rendering this woman I had never heard of into someone whose life story left tears in my eyes.

During eighty-five minutes, no interval, almost the only time she sat down was in the final minutes of the show when she lay on a sofa, asking her maid if there was any news from her children.

The ending she had agonized over was as smooth and stirring as the rest of the play. It was the applause, solely, that jerked me from my trance, and where it sent me was to my feet. Others were standing, too.

Graham clasped my shoulder. "I wouldn't have thought it at all premature to call this a phenomenal success," he said.

There were whoops and hoots all around us; the clapping went on and on. When Georgie returned for the curtain call, her eyes instantly darted in my direction. She'd probably spotted me from the start, but she was so experienced an actress that I wouldn't have known. I noticed the shiny patches under her eyes—tears she had shed for Mrs. Jordan, not in front of the audience, but in the few private moments she had backstage.

Georgie smiled at me from the stage, and for a confused moment I almost couldn't believe I was the one who had married her, shared a bed with her all those nights, had all those children with her. Tonight I was just one more theatergoer, enthralled.

There was a party afterward, and we piled into taxis to go down to a restaurant in Notting Hill. The restaurant was achingly trendy, Graham assured me, trendy to the point of having virtually no decor. There were no paintings on the walls, no plants or patterned carpets or anything but the most minimal lighting. Chocolate-brown walls, black leather chairs, white tablecloths. We filled the space with our party, and Georgie, in a cream-colored dress, glided through the room, commanding the crew as well as she did the stage. She had little presents for everybody, and red roses she handed out one by one. As she went around distributing them I could see genuine affection on the faces of those she worked with. She seemed to have gotten through this without making enemies.

I stood, of course, at the periphery, drinking a scotch, envying them all for the work they had created together and the bonds they had made while doing so. It wasn't just the creative process I missed, for even when writing had been at the center of my life, this was something I had never experienced. Writing is a solitary craft. We are always on the outside, looking in, looking longingly but never belonging, and maybe that's why we become writers, committing ourselves to a sort of sanctioned life gazing into others' brightly lit picture windows while standing in our own perpetual dusk.

Georgie appeared at my side, whispering, "Have you met them yet?" into my ear. When I shook my head she took me immediately over to Nicola, whom I found much more palatable than Georgie had suggested. She was slightly austere for my tastes, neat and small and with an overly poised manner I didn't find attractive. But many of the British women I had met seemed that way to me, a little like Wendys in the way they treated men, nannyish somehow, as if their job was to get men to behave and the only way to do this was to continually scold them. I missed in them the unlikely combination of confidence and vulnerability that I had always loved but never before named as traits of American women.

Nicola and I at first had a conversation that seemed like a parent-teacher conference; we had nothing to talk about but Georgie—her acting, her triumph that night—but after a while we got on the subject of Fanny Burney's diaries and managed a real conversation. I asked Nicola to introduce me to Piers, whom I had identified immediately from Georgie's description. He wasn't mingling but seemed instead to stand at the center of the room, waiting for people to come and speak to him.

Which everyone did, including me.

"Georgie's husband," he said, holding out his hand. "Of course. Pleasure."

"Likewise," I said, a word I was pretty sure I had never uttered aloud before.

I could see what Georgie meant about his smile. Its warmth belied the general indifference of his manner, making you want to work hard to earn it again.

My habit when I meet famous or even quasi-famous people is to make the smallest of small talk, while inside I'm dying to ask them about their music, their art, their writing. If we had been at his house I would have searched for clues to his hobbies—black-and-white photographs of his sailboat, perhaps, or his collection of jazz records— but here, with no props, I was even more limited. The smallest of small talk: the caliber of the theater, the excellent audience. He offered no challenge, and we conversed slowly and politely.

It's hard to say exactly what I thought of him. He was well-spoken, kind, heroically attentive to our dull conversation. Knowing what I know now, I would have weighed each word, each syllable, each smile or glance in her direction, I would have measured myself against him in every way possible in order to find his weaknesses, locate my comparative strengths, prepare for battle. He never asked me a single question about myself, but I didn't mind. I assumed, as I always did with famous people, that even if we met again—or again and again— the distance would remain, that we would become no closer.

It is inconceivable to me now that I could stand in a room with this man who in a matter of weeks would be fucking my wife—who probably was thinking of nothing but that as we talked—and not have a clue.

There was some glass-clinking, and then it was time for Georgie to give her speech. She stood at the front of the room in her ivory dress—like a bride, it occurred to me—cheeks flushed now from the buzz of the evening. Her speech was calculated to be warm and full of praise but not to go over the top and make everyone roll their eyes at her American sentimentality. That seemed to be the cardinal sin that an American could commit in England—the sin of overt sentimentalism.

Georgie gave the same speech I had heard her practice at home, in her pajamas, sitting cross-legged on the bed while I drank a glass of wine beside her and rested my hand on her thigh. Listening to her now I felt again what I had felt in the theater. Who was this woman? Was this really Georgie, could she still be the woman I had sometimes dreaded riding the train home to at night in New Jersey; the one who assaulted me with the litany of injustices committed upon her by her three boys and her three-bedroom raised ranch, glaring at me as if I were the gale-force wind that had knocked a tree onto our house? Was she the woman with whom I had spent evening after tedious evening bathing and diapering babies, trying to get them to eat, re-bathing the one who threw up? The woman with whom I'd made that exhausted kind of love people with small children do, the woman who kept her underpants hooked around her ankle because she'd never have the energy to fish for them at the bottom of the bed afterward?

I had forgotten what it could be like, because it had been so long since she had a role like this, one that consumed and altered her. She was my wife, but she was also someone new, a woman I had never seen before, this actress whose command of her voice and body stirred not only me but everyone in the room.

She was both; I could see that now. The new and the old live together, familiarity and surprise, the strangers in us always meeting the strangers in others, even when the others are ones we have loved.

*T*he day would come when playing Mrs. Jordan would be more like a job Georgie could show up for and do and then go home without needing to carry it with her every minute. Eventually she would be able to revel in getting up in the morning and watching the boys eat breakfast. But for now it was almost painful for her to leave the theater and come home. Home was a physical affliction, like sunburn or scar tissue, a reminder of what she was missing. She left the boys behind in all but the deepest sense when she was onstage. Because she had to—it was simple as that—she was an actor and it was part of her training.

She could leave the boys behind but she could not leave Mrs. Jordan. Not entirely—that was part of her training, too. Mrs. Jordan, actress, mistress, wife, woman of the time, talented and self-supporting, yet seduced by the power of blue blood, would stay with her throughout the run of the show, changing Georgie's life in ways that were small but perhaps permanent, leading her to a period of mourning when the show closed. It had been like that with all the parts Georgie played.

I know, because that was the way we met.

The first time I saw Georgie was at Federico's, in Murray Hill, one of those really great neighborhood restaurants that aren't fancy or expensive, just good, where you can always get a table but where every table is always filled. It was around the corner from the office where I worked three days a week to earn money while finishing my first novel. Usually I came in for lunch, but that day I had worked through lunch and knocked off early (it was that kind of job), arriving at Federico's about five-thirty with my manuscript to fiddle with while I ate alone. Georgie had worked there forever and had a seniority that allowed her to swing between lunch and dinner shifts, depending on whether she was rehearsing, performing, or theatrically unemployed. Somehow I had never crossed paths with her, or at least never noticed her, which is unlikely because Georgie is someone you notice.

That evening at Federico's, Georgie delivered a lobster platter to a table of regulars and just as she put the platter on the table, the lobster moved one of its claws. Georgie screamed and apologized, grabbed the platter, and fled to the kitchen. The entire kitchen staff was snickering, and the customers, in on the joke, were dying of laughter at the table. Understanding in an instant what had happened, Georgie punched the cook in the chest and began to cry so uncontrollably that they all gathered around to comfort her, eventually giving her the rest of the night off.

I watched, fascinated, and quickly paid my bill so that I could go out the door as she did. I invited her for a drink and it was then that I learned she was playing Laura in *The Glass Menagerie* off-off-Broadway. Laura's vulnerability had come to affect every aspect of her life, she said, and not even her coworkers, who had known her for a long time and considered her the consummate don't-fuck-with-me New Yorker, had realized it until that night.

"They're lucky I'm not doing Lady Macbeth," she told me. "I would have kicked each and every one of them in the balls. Even the women."

I suppose I fell in love with Georgie that night, the instant she burst into tears. Her splendid emotions, the rawness of it all, the way she made no apologies for what she felt or how she showed it. ("Those assholes!" she kept saying.) As we spent more time together I learned quickly to ride out the emotions, driven by the roles that seeped into her everyday life. If that is the way you fall in love, it becomes part of what you expect.

And so it was that I saw Georgie's fragile side first. If she had been playing Lady Macbeth when I met her, I don't honestly know how far the two of us would have gone.

*T*here are times, more frequent as you get older, when you are able to feel yourself utterly vanished from the life you have lived so far, an existential glimpse, perhaps—impossible within the egotistic confidence of youth—of a world based upon your absence. It can feel as raw and permanent as the truest moment of your life—and pass. A nothing. Or it can be laughable, an aberration, and yet take hold. There is no way of knowing at the time.

People used the word *blindsided*, but I would be lying if I didn't say there was a time when I presaged what I was to lose.

It is not the time you think; not when she was onstage. From years of watching her perform, I had become used to that suspension of disbelief. It was another moment, or series of identical moments, when I felt her coming into a life I no longer saw myself in.

It was this: the way she slipped quietly into the house each evening after the show, never coming straight up to bed but instead puttering downstairs, having tea in the basement kitchen, taking care of this and that, working her way up slowly, over a couple of hours, to the top of the house. She was always quiet, but I always heard her. Perhaps the boys heard her, too, because it would inevitably be during those hours that one of them would stumble into my room with an agitated "Daddy!" Most nights, when she finally made it up to our room, there was a boy on her side of the bed, usually Fergus, though sometimes Liam, almost never Jack, who slept firmly without dreams that disturbed him, and rarely woke before morning.

I understood how she felt after a performance. Her mind racing, she couldn't possibly sleep, she needed to share the show with someone in it, or someone who'd seen it, and I was neither.

The theater is rarely a lonely place—that's part of its attraction—but a one-woman show made it a lonely place for Georgie.

Annie the costume girl was twenty-one and could think of nothing but the boyfriend who was picking her up after the show. The rest of the crew had their own lives. And there was still this immense distance between Georgie and Nicola and Piers.

In our past, it had been nothing for the two of us to stay up until four a.m. after her shows, talking. She told me things then. When did she stop being the person who needed to tell me every feeling she had at the exact moment she was having it?

Maybe she would say it was about the time I started putting on a sports coat to travel on airplanes. Or maybe it was when I began to rent videos about middle-aged men who had lost their way. I suppose I was worried that our intensity had calmed, that we kept things hidden from each other—not in secretive ways, but just because we couldn't bear to open up that side of things at that particular moment. Your deepest inadequacies and fears can be told when you're young—your young frame and heart can handle it; there is deep joy in crying in each other's arms on the cheap, lumpy futon; almost everything could be fixed by making love—but when you're older you let those disappointments gestate, keeping them within because it hurts to let them out, especially to the one who loves you the most.

And I guess we don't realize how much it can cost to live that way. The price for the pleasantness is high. If you don't share the lows, it seems you might stop sharing the highs as well. And then come the small power plays that make the foundation crumble. He asks about your life and you give him no answers. You do not let him get hold of it, and then he stops trying.

Sometimes you can't talk because opening your wounds to the one who loves you more than anything is a way of wounding her, too. There's a complicity that has built up in a marriage, a complicity that is like the deal you make with yourself to forgive your own faults, to cut yourself some slack. But what you lose through such forgiveness is incredibly valuable as well.

Was I worried? I was worried about the down at the end of the up, the long descent when the show closed. These had been painful times before, and could be painful again. I dreaded these cycles, but we had been together long enough that I never worried about our marriage. The deal had been made, after all, the bargain set. There would be no big fight that could end things. She was my wife. You worry when the bad times come that you'll weather them all right, but you have learned not to leave.

And there had been this new life breathed into our marriage since coming to London. That's how it felt to me, anyway—a new life rising from the ashes of Georgie's unhappiness.

So I guess you could say I was worrying about the wrong things.

Perhaps some of the evenness, the patience, the acceptance you cultivate as you age is not wisdom and forbearance but instead inertia.

You lull yourself into thinking you are past passionate outbursts, rash, bridge-burning decisions, but then . . . You did not reckon on such strong emotions. You thought they were gone. You are a parent, you get regular sleep, you require lumbar support. You shouldn't be subject to these unpredictable emotional assaults.

But you are. And when they come, you almost welcome them because it is a way to be alive that you haven't felt in a long, long time.

And to be blindsided is literally to be hit by something that was there, following closely and to your side, all along. It is the bad marriage lying in wait for the good, the adolescence buried in complacent middle age, the rebel within the compromise.

Best to remember that life is lived not just in phases but also in layers.

I tell you: She knew I was there, waiting in our bed, and yet she did not come to me.

I am nearing the part of the story that becomes harder and harder for me to tell, the part where I must tell you what happened at the tithe barn.

I feel myself trying to stall, to stay longer in London, to tell you about the ceaseless rain of early February, to complain about Georgie's busy, crazy schedule, her exhaustion and inattentiveness, the boys' bad winter colds, their crankiness all those dark, early mornings. Those complaints are heaven-sent compared to what happened next.

The run in London was a short one, just twenty-four performances, and then, because it was a touring production, it was time to take the show on the road.

The road in England is an absurd thing, the road movie an American invention. It's only eight hundred miles from John o' Groats at the top of Scotland to the tip of Land's End. That's Chicago to New York, a trip I did on my own once, overnight, pulling a U-Haul.

England has no open road. You can credit the Romans for the few straight roads around; otherwise you are constantly twisting through narrow little towns, stopping for traffic, negotiating roundabouts.

The roundabout movie. The dual-carriageway movie.

The distances were small, but she was still going to be gone.

First there would be a five-week run in Dorset at a well-respected regional theater. The theater was in the middle of nowhere, or so it appeared on the map, but it was apparently famous, closely associated with the playwright and guaranteed a loyal local audience. The performances were clustered around the weekend; she would take the train down on Thursday mornings and return Sundays. Her time away would be minimized this way, but it would still go on for weeks. After Dorset there would be very short runs in Leeds, York, and Manchester, a few days in each town, and then they hoped to be back in London. Nicola was still trying to interest someone from the West End in a longer run—somewhere even in Haymarket or Drury Lane, where Dora Jordan herself might once have performed. She was in endless discussions with producers, but so far no one had committed to taking the play any further.

The first Dorset weekend, Georgie and the crew went down a couple of days early to rehearse in the new space. They were to be gone five nights—the longest time Georgie had spent away from the boys in their entire lives. She slipped in little comments all week to prepare them—*When I'm in Dorset and Daddy's giving you breakfast*; *When Emma tucks you in at night*; *When I talk to you on the phone at dinnertime*. No matter what she said to them, the boys appeared unconcerned, and even the morning she was to leave, they didn't seem to care at all. But when she dropped them off at their classrooms with a casual "I'll see you on Sunday morning," it was as if she had never once mentioned that she would be gone.

Jack made a noise as if he had been punched in the stomach.

"No," he said. "I don't want you to go. I want you to stay with me."

"Now, sweetheart—" she said. She rushed to head off the anxiety, but it erupted almost immediately, and he was squeezing her hand, hanging on her arm, pulling her to him. "Stay with me, stay with me, please, Mommy. Mommy, don't go."

Liam turned to face her from the doorway of his classroom. "What's importanter, your child or stupid old Mrs. Jordan?"

"Mommy has to work, sweetie," she said.

Liam kicked the wall and went into the classroom. Georgie struggled with her own emotions, that urge to say, *Fuck it, I quit,* and stay with these little boys who needed her, loved her. *Why is it,* she thought, *that you always want to run after the one that goes off in a huff, and push away the one who is clinging to you?* She tried to convince Jack to follow Liam, but he only pulled harder on her arm until it hurt. Each time she gently pushed him into the classroom he ran back out to her. Miss Arabella finally had to pick him up and hold him so that Georgie could get away. Liam stood motionless in the book corner, his back to her, while Jack writhed in Miss Arabella's arms, crying pitifully.

Only Fergus was left now, heroically patting her hand because she had tears in her eyes. "Do you *want* to go, Mommy?" he asked. "If you want to go, you should go." He kissed her hand and she held him close.

How could Dora have done this, over and over again, she wondered. How? It seemed unspeakably cruel to create these little creatures who needed you so much, so much, and then to make that need urgent and obvious and raw by leaving them, if only for a few days.

*T*he tithe barn.

The Tithe Barn Theatre, in Dorset, where Georgie would be performing *Shakespeare's Woman* for the next five weekends.

It stood in the middle of a field, far from the road and surrounded everywhere by green English meadow. No other farm buildings accompanied it, it was alone and glorious, weathered gray stones rising up from the ground to fortress-like proportions. It was called a barn, but was larger than any barn Georgie had ever seen. Its structure could not have been simpler—a long rectangle with a sloped roof, huge double doors at each end, no true windows but only narrow slits to let the light in. A pattern of small squares on the sides of the barn indicated where the medieval carpenters had placed their scaffolding to keep the heavy stone walls from collapsing as they were built.

It was of course Piers who first showed Georgie the tithe barn, wanting her to become comfortable in the space that was to serve as her theater. He picked her up from her hotel in town and drove her to the barn. The day was full of that changeable English weather that so exasperated Georgie; she could see six different kinds of sky from the car. It wasn't a long drive, and they reached the barn in a few minutes. Except for a small weathered sign at the turnoff from the road, there was no indication that this medieval barn was now used as a theater.

Approaching the barn on foot after they had parked the car, Georgie felt as if she were entering a cathedral. It was that big, it was that impressive.

Inside, the scale of the barn took hold of her immediately, its beautiful dim emptiness sliced only by the weakest of sunlight coming through the thin lancet windows. Posts ran down the center of the barn, and an intricate structure of roof timbers rose upward from the tops of the thick stone walls. They were there to hold up the roof, yet the curve and arch created in doing so was the greater gift to the soul. It seemed improbable that these graceful pieces of wood should be able to hold up the heavy stone of the walls and the roof, improbable that what appeared from outside as a gray monolith could be dependent on something so prone to rot and weakness as wood. Georgie stared at the magnificent roof, the beams curved and entwining like some sort of inverted altar. She had no idea why these pieces of wood should move her so, but they did.

"I should have prepared you more for the space," Piers told her after he brought her in.

"Yes," Georgie whispered. "No, it's okay. I love it."

"It is lovely, isn't it? Come, I'll take you through."

Together they walked the length of the barn, wide and empty, to the end that was used as a theater. A small wooden stage and a couple of hundred chairs stood there, but in the immensity of the barn it appeared to be nothing more than a pile of furniture pushed aside for a dance.

"Believe it or not," Piers said, studying her face, "there are actually more seats here than in London. But the proportions—"

"The proportions are huge," Georgie said. "Why would they build something like this just for some cows and pigs?"

"You can't compare this to the wooden barns you have in America, my dear. Our English weather is mild, you see, we don't need to keep our animals indoors. A tithe barn was built only to store the grain that the Church required as tithes."

"The offering, you mean? Grain instead of money?"

"Not offering," Piers corrected. "Tax. The tithe barn was a sort of bank for the local abbey. The Church ran practically everything in the Middle Ages, you know, not just religion but education, record keeping, often medicine. They needed money for all that, and this is where they collected it. Money, in the form of grain."

"So people just brought in piles of their grain and heaped it up in the barn?" Georgie asked.

"Something like that," Piers said. "Each paid in accordance with the size of his land, a tithe generally being ten percent of the yield."

Georgie continued walking the perimeter of the barn, and Piers stayed beside her. The barn was no less than a cathedral; she could feel her feet outlining the shape of a cross.

"And it wasn't really a religious building at all?" she asked.

"No, not in its use, though it was built and maintained by the Church. Often the barn would be the first thing built in a new parish so they could collect enough tithes to go on to build the abbey."

"How old is it?"

"Late thirteenth, early fourteenth century, maybe. We don't know for certain."

"It's amazing," Georgie said. "This was ancient even in Mrs. Jordan's time. She could have come here."

"There's nothing that places her in Dorset, but yes, the barn certainly was here during her lifetime. I can't say it went anywhere." He smiled at her. They had stopped near the stage. She had never lost her self-consciousness around Piers and was grateful to have a steady stream of questions to ask.

"When was it turned into a theater?"

"The mid-eighties," Piers said. "That was my doing, I confess. I had this vision. A great countryside theater. I dreamed of a place where people could come from all the local villages and circle their cars round and see a performance worthy of London. Fortunately I was able to convince Thurrock I knew what I was talking about."

"Thurrock?"

"He's the landowner. You'll meet him at some point, I expect. He wasn't too keen at first on doing a conversion. He wanted to maintain the integrity of the barn." Piers paused and swept his gaze up the long stone walls. "As did I. We made no changes to the structure at all, really. The main problem, of course, was fenestration."

"Of course," Georgie said, frowning. "What the hell's fenestration?"

"Windows," Piers said. "The lancet windows are so lovely, but they let in so damn little light, and the Council gets nervous when you start talking about knocking holes in the side of a seven-hundred-year-old building. We had to put in a fantastically expensive lighting system. It took years to do what we did, but it's been worth it. It's become quite well known, this theater. You'll see. Everybody comes. But there's no such thing as a sellout. We simply bring out more chairs." He smiled at what was clearly an amusing point of pride for him.

"What would have happened to it if you hadn't turned it into a theater?" Georgie asked.

Piers shrugged. "Hard to say. The National Trust might have taken an interest in it, or it might just be sitting here storing Thurrock's collection of old cars."

"I love it. The roof structure especially," Georgie said, wincing at how inarticulate she sounded. How American next to Piers's elegant vocabulary of medievalism.

Georgie stood to one side of the barn and took in the ancient, silent space. She was trying to imagine herself performing there. *All theater is a response to architecture,* a director had once told her, and in the tithe barn she was already starting to feel a change in Mrs. Jordan.

"Something this beautiful just to dump grain in," she said softly.

Piers pointed to the beams rising from the side of the wall. "It's the internal frame that holds up the roof, you see, not the walls. Heavy as they are, the walls bear very little weight. The wood is pushed to its absolute limit. It carries the whole load of the roof on those thin timbers. It's all down to the astonishing tensile capabilities of the wood."

He turned back to Georgie and gave her a wry smile. "I'm sorry. This barn is a passion of mine."

"I can tell," she said. She smiled back, and as it became obvious to both of them that they were staring at each other, she began to laugh nervously.

"Oh, look, here's Nicola," Piers said, and Georgie gratefully turned away from Piers.

The rehearsal went badly. Very badly.

Georgie warmed to the acoustics in no time, but the physicality of herself on the tithe barn stage after the intimacy of the studio theater in London threw her off. The early scenes were all right, but as Mrs. Jordan aged, her life becoming fraught with conflicts and anxieties, Georgie could feel herself overpitching her performance. She did it because she felt herself getting smaller and smaller on the stage.

Nicola and Piers threw up their hands in a way they never had in London. Georgie felt like a petulant three-year-old whose parents were trying to get her to perform in a ballet recital or school play.

Piers spent a lot of time frowning. "Let's take a break," Nicola said at one point, going out for a brisk walk, and leaving Georgie and Piers to sit in chairs and stare despondently at the empty stage.

"It's the space," she told him.

"I thought you liked the space."

"I do. I love the space. It's just that for me it brings up the whole issue of the ending again. The ending is even more out of place here than in London."

Piers turned to her and spoke sharply. "May I please say that it's not possible after all those performances in London to carry on about the ending?"

"No, you may not 'please say,'" Georgie said, equally sharply. "It's possible. I'm doing it. Hear me carrying on?"

"I most certainly do hear you."

"Just let me show you how it should be. I'm not telling you how to rewrite your play—"

"That's exactly what you're doing."

"Just let me show you," she said. "In this space it's even more of a surrender for me," Georgie said. "For *her*, I mean. She's lost. You can't ask her to command this space and then give herself up to it at the end."

"The play has a sad ending," Piers said. "You should be proud of all those tears you've drawn in London."

"I'm not proud," Georgie said, "because she shouldn't get those tears. She should triumph over the audience. This woman had thirteen children. She went on night after night, during wars, during her children's illnesses, her own illnesses, even with a broken heart. She wasn't afraid to speak to the audience when they gave her shit—"

"You've fallen in love," Piers said softly. He was smiling now, all traces of irritation gone.

"Excuse me?"

"With Mrs. Jordan. I did, too. That's why I wrote the play."

"I just need to show you," Georgie said.

She took her place onstage, on the chaise longue, and lowered her head for a moment. When she snapped her head back she said,

I grow weaker, so that I can scarcely rise from this sofa. The French doctor has been to see me. He calls it jaundice, la maladie noire.

Past twelve and still no letters, Miss Sketchley? Would you please go into the village and check again?

It is not, believe me, the feelings of pride, avarice, or the absence of those comforts I have all my life been accustomed to, that is killing me by inches; it is the loss of my only remaining comfort, the hope I used to live on from time to time, of seeing my children.

That was the play's ending, but Georgie went on, pulling herself up from the chaise longue to begin a speech by Viola that she knew by heart.

Too well what love women to men may owe:
In faith, they are as true of heart as we.
My father had a daughter loved a man
As it might be, perhaps, were I a woman,
I should your Lordship.

And what's her history?

A blank, my lord. She never told her love,
But let concealment, like a worm i' the bud,
Feed on her damask cheek. She pined in thought,
And with a green and yellow melancholy
She sat like Patience on a monument,
Smiling at grief. Was not this love indeed?
We men may say more, swear more, but indeed
Our shows are more than will; for still we prove
Much in our vows but little in our love.

Georgie raised her arms and face as if she were basking in the glow of God or the sun.

The applause. Miss Williams, do you hear it? Oh, what internal exulta-
tion animates the form and stimulates the senses. It has always been a
delight for me, a delight that borders on ecstasy.

She stood silently for a moment, letting Mrs. Jordan flow away. His eyes were fixed.

Nothing is as attractive as talent.

Not youth, not beauty.

Nothing.

She was alone on the stage and then suddenly he was there, too, stepping forward from his seat to stand within inches so that when she lowered her face he was able to kiss her.

She did not immediately register the kiss, which was long and hard, unhurried, forceful yet at the same time undemanding. He was giving her the kiss, asking, it seemed, for nothing in return. She hadn't yet come out of character, and her reaction was not of shock or anger but of surprise—was he kissing Mrs. Jordan or was he kissing her? She neither drew back nor returned the kiss but instead simply stared into his eyes, directly opposite her own.

"You are amazing," he said, running one finger down her cheek.

"Please," she said.

"Yes," he said, "please."

Her children were far away, her husband at work in London. She loved them, but for the moment they were not real to her, and she was left alone with this writer who wanted her. The expanse of the barn opened up a world that was new to her, but she stepped back and left it, for the moment, at the kiss.

*T*hursday night's performance went better than its rehearsal had predicted, but the audience was tepid. Nicola had many comments afterward, and Georgie listened, glassy-eyed and nodding. She avoided Piers, retreating to her hotel room as quickly as she could. She had her usual postperformance manic energy, but on top of that was no small amount of shame, a certain lurking danger, the clambering scent of excitement.

It was easy for Georgie to tell herself that the kiss was an aberration. Very easy. How many kisses had she given and received in her career? Passionate kisses, deep tongue kisses, because a theater was so small everyone could tell if you faked it. Kisses that had to convince hundreds of people you were in love, in lust, desperate for the man in your arms.

It was a stage kiss. Wasn't it on a stage, wasn't she still in character?

She could link the kiss with the stage, and except when she relived it, it could be forgotten.

But a kiss is enough to set things in motion. It is enough to spiral the energy of resistance, turn it toward the realm of the possible. *I couldn't. I couldn't possibly. No, never. I can't—*

I am.

⸙

She lay in bed that night thinking of the kiss, of Piers, of what had happened between them and what might still happen if she let it. But why, why let it? She had no reason to. She had not been looking for another man. She couldn't think of it. She had to stop. She tried to picture only me, and the boys, but what also entered her head, without warning or context as she worked her way back to sleep, was the face of an old friend from New York, an old male friend, Lewis, whom she loved and whom she hadn't seen in several years. He had moved to Los Angeles about the time we moved to New Jersey, but for years before that, for years and years, they had met almost monthly to see a film or a play or have dinner together. He was her friend, one of those people who hadn't ever become really *my* friend, *our* friend, though he was just a friend, never a lover; in fact he was gay.

It can't always have been winter when she met him, but in her memory it was winter and she could feel the blast of warmth as they descended the escalator from the chilly air into the movie theater near Lincoln Center to see the latest French film and gossip about the theater world. She could recall the exact scratchy feel of the angora scarf she had worn for a number of years, the worn green coat with the hole in the silk of the left pocket. It represented a very long time in her life, that friendship with Lewis, it went on for years and years. She had expected to grow old still meeting him for dinner, two old actors getting together in the same old places to talk about much the same things.

Now that they were so far apart, Georgie and Lewis carried on an occasional but devoted correspondence. They sent each other these friend-love letters scribbled on art postcards with pretty quotes. She had not written to him since moving to England—he knew nothing of Mrs. Jordan—and her eyes teared up with missing him.

It was nothing more than an ache for the part of her life when she and Lewis had known each other so well in New York, and yet she found it odd that she should be thinking so passionately of him. The mind is incredibly accomplished at deflecting what is at its center, forcing you instead to look at something similar yet less terrifying to contemplate.

Knowing she was going to do what she had decided not to do had filled her with mighty longing for yet another of the lives she had left behind.

When she was able to sleep she slept well, but awoke at five the next morning, heart racing from the various anxieties battling for her attention. She had the whole day off—Nicola had decided that they would gain nothing by having another run-through of the show, so Georgie was to relax, "have a lie-in," simply enjoy her day until the six-thirty call that evening.

She didn't know what to do with all that time. For a moment she thought of taking the train back to London, rushing to the school to hug her sons, finding me and making me stop her from doing what she now surely might do.

No, there wasn't enough time to make it to London and back before the curtain.

Friday was the town's market day, and the stalls opened at seven. She made her way the short distance from the railway hotel to the village square, carrying a tote bag, looking out for things she thought the boys might like. It was then that she missed them the most, which was silly because they were in school and wouldn't have been with her anyway. But she kept trying to imagine the boys beside her, helping to count vegetables, choose fresh flowers, find pretty new tea towels and oven mitts to replace the faded, stained ones we used at home. In fact, if Fergus, Liam, and Jack had been there it would have been nothing so idyllic. There would have been fighting, there would have been many wants, many nos, a moment's disappearance or two. The only time most of us want more children is when the ones we have are angelically asleep. Or somewhere else, being well looked after.

As she walked through the market, looking at linens and spices and little wooden toys, her anxieties began to lessen slightly, and it comforted her that she could pare her existence down to just this: a woman strolling the narrow streets of a pretty English village.

Mid-morning, she stopped at a tearoom down one of the streets off the market square. She didn't even bother to buy a newspaper—that would bring the world back before her, and for now that didn't seem necessary. All she wanted to do was sit at an impossibly small round table, her purchases on the chair across from her, have tea and scones, and contemplate the lives of the people passing by the window.

That must be the key to Mrs. Jordan, she thought when, refreshed, she was back at the market again: within all her complicated comings and goings, tending to family and love affair, playing her roles, and managing the business side of her career, Mrs. Jordan was able to have moments like this, too, moments of peace in which she could separate herself from everyone who knew and loved and demanded and obligated her, and discover in those moments—rare, decidedly rare—that she knew who she was.

"Georgie?"

Her hand immediately went to her face. No makeup. Dirty hair because clean hair was too slippery, wouldn't hold the pin curls she needed to wear under her wigs that evening.

There, buying sausages and big wedges of cheese, was Piers.

"Hello," she said. "Good morning."

"You're an early riser." Predictable words, cliché beyond cliché, yet coming out of his mouth they sounded almost clever.

"Not usually," she said.

"Are you finding everything you need here in our little market?"

She weakly lifted her bag. As if for the first time, he seemed to realize that she might have some time on her hands.

"I've nearly finished with my shopping," he said. "Why don't you come round for a cup of tea?"

She weighed his words carefully. Did "Come round for a cup of tea" mean the same thing as "Come up for a drink" did in America? She felt safe there in the crowded market square but knew how vulnerable she might become if she were alone with Piers once again.

"No," she said slowly. "No thank you."

"Are you certain? I've nothing on all day. I can—"

"No, thanks," Georgie said, insistent this time. "I've got some shopping to do still. I want to buy some things for my kids."

"All right," Piers said, his gaze resting on her. "But if you change your mind, meet me at the fruit stall in a half-hour. It's not far to my place, and I'm quite happy to bring you back to the hotel later."

"That's okay," Georgie said. She turned away from him abruptly, almost rudely, and walked toward a cutlery stall as if it were her intended destination. She stood there for a few minutes, not really looking at the knives and kitchen tools displayed, trying desperately to subdue her heart's urgent beating.

She knew she should go back to the hotel. Straight back. Stay there until it was time for the show. Make sure that she was never alone with Piers, that Nicola or the stage manager or the entire audience was there to stand between them. This could be like so many of the attractions she had felt in her stage life—brief, a little silly, a little fun, unrequited.

But she didn't want it to be that way. She wanted him, this man, wanted to get closer and closer and closer to him, wanted to be drawn in, taken apart, put back together again with the expertise she knew he possessed. She felt she could not take another step in any direction except toward him. She needed, at that moment in her life, nothing and no one but him.

"Can I help you, luv?" the man at the cutlery stall asked, and she could muster no words, only a shake of her head. She turned from the glinting stainless-steel blades and walked toward the Bramley apples and Comice pears, the blackberries and imported satsumas. Piers waited for her there.

The pace of her heartbeat quickened again as she approached. She had almost decided to turn back when he spotted her.

"Oh, good," he said so calmly that she almost resented him for it. "Fancied some company after all."

He pointed down one of the roads leading away from the square and said, "See, my cottage is just—that way."

The sidewalk was too narrow to walk side by side, and Georgie followed him awkwardly until the town seemed abruptly to end and it appeared as if they were suddenly in the wilderness. After a few more minutes of walking, they reached his small stone house.

"Come in," he said, opening the door without unlocking it. "Tea? Coffee?"

"Tea would be great." She followed him into the kitchen, where he filled the electric kettle with water and put teabags into two bright blue mugs. The cottage was very small inside, just an open-plan living room with a kitchen and a loftlike ladder leading upstairs. Georgie spied his desk in front of the window, neatly piled with papers and books.

"Is this where you do your writing?" she asked.

"Some of it," he said. "I wrote most of *Shakespeare's Woman* here. The singularity of the view was pleasing. I needed to be inside her head. London's something else entirely. I love going up to London, but I need a view like this if I'm going to work."

Georgie walked over to the picture window over his desk and looked outside. "How long have you lived here?" she asked.

"Nearly all my life, really. We came down from London for school holidays, many weekends. Merry weekends. Lately I find myself spending more and more time here. I'm a great lover of the countryside."

Georgie, who was not a great lover of the countryside, said, stiffly, "It is very pretty."

Piers shrugged. "I've often thought that there is something, I don't know, agricultural about being a playwright. A wright. A wainwright, a wheelwright, a playwright. The craft of it is appealing, as if I'm just tinkering with words out here."

Georgie heard cautious footsteps coming down the ladder, and she thought, *There's someone else here.* She felt a brief but surprisingly bitter moment of disappointment followed very quickly by relief. Someone else was there. Nothing was to happen.

"Would you like a cup of tea, Mrs. Parr?" Piers asked, and a woman who was obviously there to clean the house appeared.

"No thank you, Mr. Brighstone. I've nearly finished my work."

"Mrs. Parr, this is Georgina Connolly. Shakespeare's Woman."

"Oh, lovely." Mrs. Parr held out her hand. "I'm seeing the show tomorrow. The matinee."

"Thank you," Georgie murmured.

"See?" Piers said. "I told you. Everybody knows about it. Everybody goes. Lucky for you, Mrs. Parr has a very large family."

Georgie and Piers sat at the table and drank their tea.

"Would you like an orange?" Piers asked, and when Georgie nodded he began to peel one for her. He handed her the fresh wedges, and they tasted better than any orange she could ever remember tasting. She and Piers said little to each other, and their time was made even more awkward by Mrs. Parr popping in and out of the room with armloads of washing or a bucket of cleaning supplies.

Finally Piers said, "Let's take a walk out to the tithe barn. It's not far. Actually, we're on the same parcel of land. It's really worth doing. You'll get an incomparable view of the barn on the approach."

He led her to the back door, where the washing machine and dryer hummed away and a collection of coats hung on pegs on the walls. "You'll need to borrow a pair of wellies," Piers said, opening a shoe cupboard. "I'm afraid it's still terribly muddy."

She took off her shoes and slid her feet into the green boots he offered her.

In the time it took them to cross the field to the barn, the sky changed from overcast to bright blue with beautiful backlit gray clouds. It was something Georgie could not get used to. In New York you could look out the window when you woke up in the morning and say, *It's a beautiful day, we can have a picnic this afternoon,* or, *It's raining, let's go to the museum.* Here you could have beautiful moments, rainy patches, and the weather could transform utterly in the time it took to propel yourself across a small field.

"This was all part of the same estate at one time," Piers said. "Mine was the north gatehouse, the less showy one. Hence my family's ability to afford it."

"I thought this was the Church's land."

"It was, until Thurrock's family got hold of it. It's been in his family since the dissolution."

"Dissolution?"

"Of the monasteries."

"Oh, right. That was part of the whole Church of England thing, right? Henry the Eighth wanted a divorce . . ."

"The dissolution was a little later, actually, but Henry the Eighth was the culprit behind that as well. The Church's landholdings were vast, and he wanted it all for the crown."

"Why?"

Piers shrugged. "Who knows?" he said. "He was the king. Kings want things. He granted some land as favors, sold lots of it. Actually, by the end of his reign he'd sold off two-thirds of it to pay for the expensive wars he was fighting. It's not that he created scores of new landowners. Most estates were bought by people who already had money. Those with land and money acquired more, and those without got nothing."

"Just like now."

"Thurrock's ancestors were already quite wealthy when they bought this estate. Things didn't get grim for them until much later. When Thurrock inherited all this after World War Two, he found he had to make some money, so he opened the house to the public. You can tour it for eight pounds fifty if you like."

"Is it worth it?"

"Absolutely not. It's the traditional three or four rooms open, laid out with ancestral portraits and Thurrock's witty commentary about their zany antics. There's a little train to take you from one part of the estate to the other. The usual tearooms and gift shop, and I heard he's put in an aviary and an adventure playground as well."

"Maybe that's what I'll do on my next day off."

They walked on and Piers said, "The abbey stood around here somewhere. I'm not precisely sure where. Nothing's left of it, not even ruins. The tithe barn is the only abbatial building extant."

"Impressive," Georgie said.

"I know," Piers said.

"Not the barn. You. The way you can say 'abbatial' like that. Abbatial, abbatial . . . No wonder we don't stand a chance around the English."

Piers smiled. "They deroofed the abbeys during the dissolution, but they didn't bother with the tithe barns. They could serve a useful secular purpose for the new owner."

"Why did they deroof the abbeys?"

"That's all it took to send them to ruin. Plus, the lead from the roofs was quite valuable."

"What happened to the monks?"

"Most of them were not that broken up about it. Numbers were dwindling, anyway. Britain was a fairly secular country even then,

Henry the Eighth just helped it along. There's nothing to suggest there were homeless monks running round the countryside. Some found work elsewhere in the Church. The nuns met with worse luck, I'm afraid. They were literally forced to depend on charity. Some married, because what else was open to a woman in the sixteenth century? This was before they were even allowed to be actresses. Henry the Eighth had in effect removed one of the only two career options for women."

By the time they reached the barn, it had begun to rain, and Piers unlocked the door quickly.

"It has a holy feel, this place," Georgie said once they were inside, shaking themselves dry. She looked up at the ceiling and Piers stood behind her.

He said, "What I love is the spatial unity. It seems to be one piece of material, not hundreds of little timbers."

"It's hard to believe that wood can hold this building up," Georgie said.

"You have to think how long this building has stood here, for thirty or so generations, and has changed barely at all." His voice was close to her ear, close enough that she could feel his breath. She hadn't heard his voice in her ear before. All these weeks Nicola had been too close to her on the stage, Nicola's voice had invaded her thoughts, but Piers had never been this close except for once, in this barn, just two days ago, when he had first kissed her.

She knew if she turned around he would kiss her again.

"Tell me," she said instead. "Are you and Nicola lovers?"

"We were once," he answered.

"And now?"

"And now we're colleagues."

"Were you lovers when you picked her to direct your play?"

"Why does that matter?"

"I just wondered if you thought she was the best director for *Shakespeare's Woman* or whether it was a project the two of you wanted to work on together because you *were* together."

He was quiet.

"So you're not going to tell me?" she asked.

"I'm trying to remember."

"You're being very evasive," Georgie said. "Maybe a little cadlike."

"Perhaps I should return to reciting 'abbatial,'" Piers said.

"Perhaps."

And that was when she turned around.

*T*he maid gone, the bed newly made with fresh white sheets—there was no doubt where they were headed from the moment they returned to his house. But they never made it to the bed.

They never made it to the bed.

He kissed her just inside the door as she stood up after pulling off her boots.

"Piers." She called him by his name for what may have been the first time. He kissed her again, smelling like the rain and the old stone barn they had come from, but also like some warm memory of a promise someone once made to her in a dream about what her life would be. His hands, which had barely touched her skin before, lay warm against her cheeks and smelled still of the freshly peeled orange. They stroked her neck and then traveled down to her waist, reaching under her shirt to seek out her breasts. The steady perfect cups of his hands on her breasts made her gasp. He undid her bra strap and bent quickly to get his lips around one of her nipples. His hands moved down the curves of her body, and she was kissing him as if they were teenagers in her parents' hallway with only minutes before they might be discovered.

Except they didn't need to be quiet, and they weren't. They were in his house in the middle of the countryside, and Piers, always so quiet in speech, was now talking endlessly: "You're so beautiful, Georgie. Georgie, I want you so much."

And her hands sought out his skin, too, his chest, his arms, all as warm as the hands that were now unbuttoning her jeans, sliding deeply down under her pants.

"Oh God," he said in her ear as soon as he touched below the hair to the hairless folds, the slippery moist lobes that wanted his fingers.

They didn't even get to the bed. Fuck the bed, the nice clean sheets, fuck the trip up the ladder to the loft—they were almost naked by the back door. He pulled her jeans off so that he could sit between the V of her legs and bury his face there. He licked her and she crouched, accommodating him, one hand clutching at the washing machine for balance. She spread her legs farther and farther so she could feel the tip of his tongue inside her like a pointed flame. And when she came—when she came—he held her up as she flounced and jerked, and then he let her fall gently on top of him. She groped at his belt, trembling, and he pulled off his pants and stood up, and she was lying on her stomach so he did not bother to turn her over but came into her from behind so he could hold on to her breasts while he slammed into her there against the washing machine.

"Oh, sweet," he said, and when he came, "Oh, Georgie."

*H*ow do I know? How can I possibly know?

Some of the most important scenes in our lives are ones we do not witness.

I knew because I wanted to know, I had to know. And she, during hours and days of talk and fights and crying and screaming and threats—she told me. Maybe she thought by giving me all of it, by honestly answering every single question, by telling me exactly what I wanted to know, she would somehow be able to keep me. Because she did tell me everything, and when I asked for more she gave me that, too, until I could get hold of the five or six details to store up in precise word and image in order to torture myself again and again.

She had been tempted before.

I had been tempted before.

A morning after a party I searched for a CD I had not listened to in years and then played a single track over and over again the entire weekend. Who was it, she wondered, who had made me need to hear that song?

A small role in Shakespeare in the Park, a Richard III she had idolized since she was a girl—he invited her back to his place one night after the show, but she said no, rushing home to make love to me instead.

It's not temptation alone, or chance. And it is not a moment, because it takes more than a moment to find a place to go, to take off your clothes. It involves momentum, the strength of a moment sustained.

What would you do, what would you risk, to feel that way? To feel that thrill once again, after so many years, of not knowing what was going to happen the very next minute?

I know nothing about you," she said to him as they lay in bed. "Don't you think I should know more about you?" He had come to her room after the Friday show, and now here they were again between the Saturday matinee and evening performances. They didn't discuss it; he had simply shown up at her door and she had been waiting for him.

"What would you like to know?" he asked amiably.

"Your birthday, for one."

"June 17, 1956. And?"

"And everything else," she said. "Your life story."

"Well."

"I wouldn't be surprised to find out you had children."

"I have children."

"And?"

"And?"

"How many, how old. God, you're so unforthcoming."

"They're twenty-six and twenty-seven."

"Where do they live?"

"In London, both of them."

"And their mother?"

"She lives in London, too."

"Stop it," Georgie said. "You're doing it on purpose."

"Look, there's not much to say, really. Henrietta and I married very young. We divorced almost twenty-five years ago. She remarried, and James and Hayley were really raised by Henrietta and her new husband."

"What happened?"

"When?"

"To your marriage."

"Oh. Henrietta wanted to live in Fulham and have dinner parties. I needed to go days without talking to anyone."

"So you left them all?"

"I was asked to leave."

"You were asked? Meaning, she wouldn't play by your rules and you wouldn't change, so . . ."

"Something like that. Marriage and art aren't terribly compatible."

"I don't get it," Georgie said.

"What?"

"How you could have written this beautiful play about this warm, vibrant woman and yet be so cold."

"I wouldn't have said I was cold."

"I would have," Georgie said. "Oh boy would I have said it. In fact I *am* saying it. Cold." She pressed one finger against his arm. "See? Chilly. Brrr."

She didn't know him. And yet maybe that was what appealed to her. Georgie was a woman with three brothers. A husband. Three sons. A beloved father. Mostly male friends. If there's anything she knew, it was men. She would not for a moment have described them as enigmatic, mysterious, puzzling. But here was a man who was foreign to her, whom she didn't immediately understand. And there was this fading smile on his face—perhaps he was as cold as she was saying he was. She had a mild feeling of wanting to get away from him, but of not wanting that to happen anytime soon, of first wanting to borrow, or take from him what she needed for herself, for her own work and life. She needed him now as much as she needed Mrs. Jordan, as much as Mrs. Jordan needed Rosalind.

*A*fter Saturday evening's show, Nicola pulled Georgie aside. "I thought it was just last night," she said, "but you did it again today, Georgie. Something quite different is happening up there. I have to say you've really gone from strength to strength with this role."

"Thank you."

"Listen," Nicola continued, "I'm doing some preproduction work on a new show, and it would really suit me to stay in London all week. It's going so well I thought I might not bother coming down next weekend. You don't really seem to need me, do you?"

"No," Georgie said evenly.

"Obviously Piers is here and the crew, if there are emergencies," Nicola told Georgie, "but I honestly can't foresee any problems."

Piers came in then, and leaned against the door frame to listen.

"I think we can survive without you, my dear," he said.

Georgie looked furtively at Piers. His gaze was open, entirely open, entirely directed at her. She knew little more about this man than she had when she first met him, but now his presence held her in a way she hadn't been held in a long time.

She took an early train home Sunday morning, then a taxi, her steps aching for us as she raced toward the house. Liam spied her from the window and opened the front door, something he was forbidden to do, but she didn't bother to scold him.

He was there.

We were all still there.

The blue carpeting snapped at her senses, her arms took in as much of us as she could.

"Mom, you got here very fast," Fergus said. "Much faster than the speed of light."

"We got a video," Liam said.

"*Lassie!*" Jack shouted.

"I was going to say!" Liam said. "I was supposed to say!" He elbowed Jack in the ribs, and Jack started to cry.

"Liam," I said. "Tell your brother you're sorry."

Liam shut his eyes tightly and put his fingers in his ears. "Sorry sorry sorry sorry sorry," he whispered while Jack played the victim, curling in Georgie's lap on the floor before she could even get her coat off.

"God, I love these children," she said to me, raising her eyes above Jack's burrowing head, trying to meet mine. *What am I doing,* she thought. *What the hell am I doing.*

"Welcome home," I said, and kissed her.

She would end it. She would not keep this going, this thing that had barely started. Unlike so many people who find themselves standing inside an unhappy marriage, with a husband they can't talk to, hostile walls and furniture closing in on them, saying, *This is not my life,* Georgie was comforting herself, wrapping herself around it, saying, with gratitude, *Yes, this is my life.* She would claim it back before anyone even found out she had put it at risk.

In the afternoon, while the boys watched the video, she showered and then we made love. That was her impulse, not to distance her body but to lay further claim to mine. She had slept with Piers only twice, but with me there had been thousands of nights, twelve years of nights and, until now, no one else.

She knew my body so well, by feel, by taste. That mole on my chest that always fooled her into thinking it was my left nipple, always, until she moved her hand farther along. The small round indentation on the back of my left upper arm that was my smallpox vaccination. The concave place on my chest, at the center of my ribcage, just large enough to rest her palm.

She lay against me and fell asleep, waking afterward with a gasp.

"What?" I asked. "Did you have a 'day stallion'?"

She smiled at this phrase, coined by Fergus, who thought if a bad dream at night was a nightmare, a bad dream in the daytime must be a day stallion.

"God," she said. "Peter, they've been down there almost two hours on their own."

"Do you suppose we should check for survivors?"

"I'll go," she said.

She pulled on her robe and took the steps quickly, slowing as she reached the door of the sitting room. She wanted to catch them by surprise, to have her heart break at the sincere little shape of their heads before they saw her.

All was quiet, very quiet, but on the couch, Jack's shoulders were shaking, and she let her steps get louder, preparing to yell at the other two boys for making him cry. Before she could say anything, Fergus went up and put his arm around him, saying, "Don't cry, Jacky. You can tell by the music Lassie's going to be all right."

She slipped away without being seen, returning upstairs to me. The bed was warm, the sheets smelled like us, I was there reaching for her. Her face was dotted with round warm tears that stayed there like raindrops on a windshield.

"I love you," she whispered, and until I knew better, that afternoon stayed with me as one of the finest we had known in some time.

Oh, Georgie, weren't there already enough of us who adored you? Why did you need one more?

She did not see him all week in London. She saw me, and the children. She took them to the science museum after school. She took them to tea. She ironed their white school shirts as penance; she took my shoes to the repair shop. She would be a good wife. She would be a good mother.

But there was this other thing—that she could have done this without anyone knowing. No one. After years of the communal experience that was family life, especially for a mother, she had a private life again, and she walked around with the secret, dangerous euphoria she had carried when she was first pregnant and had told no one yet, not even me.

Because it had not entered the life of the family, it had barely happened.

It hadn't happened.

And yet she had not simply walked to the line, she had crossed it, and now she found she wanted nothing more than to stand in her cramped basement kitchen and help the boys with their reading. Just stand there serving up chicken nuggets.

She would be a good wife. She would be a good mother.

For me, the week was indistinguishable from the weeks that preceded and followed it, but when I cast my eyes back over it now there are details, escapes from the expected, things I might have seen if I had bothered to look. At the time I was so busy looking only at the edges of Georgie's life—the pieces that fit into mine, those bits that joined to our family—that I did not bother to see what was at its center.

She came with me to a client dinner, a black-tie evening at the V&A. It was the kind of thing that never happened in New York— the magazine was far too cheap—but in trying to break into the European market they were spending a little money for once. They hired a band, laid out an expensive spread. The chairman had flown in from New York.

"Well," he said to Georgie, "I guess Pete will be turning in his resignation now that his wife's a famous actress." He was red-faced from wine and a little sweaty, trying to pull himself up to Georgie's height.

"Hardly," Georgie said.

"I suppose you'll be dragging him off to Hollywood next. He won't need to be a hack reporter anymore." He laughed in a way that sounded exactly like "heh heh heh."

"Did you see the show?" Georgie asked.

"Not yet. I hear great things about it, though. Great things."

"I see," she said.

"My wife—" he said, by way of apology, or excuse, and Georgie frowned. It was one of her pet peeves, people who insisted on talking to her about her career, assuming they knew something about it when they did not even have the decency to buy a ticket to the show. No matter how broke she was, she saw the show, bought the book, went to the gallery opening. It stemmed from one of her father's famous sayings: *If you know the guy who's singing the song*, he always said, *for the love of God, listen to the song.*

I could see she was ready to launch into it with the chairman—my boss's boss's boss—which might not have been the best thing for my career, so I stepped in.

"Would you like to dance?" I asked her.

"But of course," she said, smiling. In whose voice? Greta Garbo's? Bette Davis's?

And we danced.

We rarely danced and weren't particularly good together, though Georgie had had lots of dance and movement classes over the years. Nonetheless it felt good to dance, to be touching each other.

"I want you back," I said.

"What do you mean?" she asked quickly, no Greta Garbo voice this time.

"I mean 'back,'" I said. "As opposed to 'away'? I've missed you."

"I've missed you, too," she said. She clasped my neck tighter, relieved that my comment was pure innocence. Of course, she realized, there was no need to worry. She had almost forgotten. She could do what she liked: I trusted her.

A s for the boys, they were so happy to have their mother home that they made it a point to forget she had to leave again in four days' time. When Georgie tucked Fergus into bed the night before her return to Dorset, his eyes teared and he rubbed at them furiously. "I don't want you to go," he said. "I want you to stay with me."

"I can't stay, sweetie." She smiled at him gently, and smoothed the spiky hairs at the crown of his head, the ones that would never lie down. She wondered if this would ever get any easier, or if she would always feel her heart tearing into shreds each time the boys pleaded with her not to go. I'm their mother, she thought, they need me. But she was also remembering the weightlessness, and the sheer joy at the weightlessness, that she felt once she was actually gone.

"Then I'll come with you," Fergus said.

"You have to go to school."

"Dumb old school." He turned his face and she saw two tears drop on his pillow.

"I'll tell you what I can do, though," Georgie said, filling her voice with excitement and conspiracy—a secret just between the two of them. "I can bring you something. A present. What would you like me to bring you?"

While pausing to think, he seemed to get hold of himself for a moment. "If you see some nice shirts, then buy one for me," he said brightly, before crumbling into a pathetic little sob, "in—my—size."

She stayed with him for a time, rubbing his back and waiting for him to sleep. When his fidgeting eventually died down, she heard regular breathing and lifted herself gently out of his bed.

"No, Mommy, no," he said.

"Can't I go now?" she asked.

"No," he said. "Never." Then, "Check on me. Keep checking on me. Every minute."

"Okay," she said, moving quietly out of the room.

"Every minute."

As soon as she was in the hallway he called out, "I changed my mind. I changed my mind, Mommy." He sounded alarmed, and she hurried back into the room.

"Sssh," she said, afraid he would wake the other two. She tried to negotiate. "How about if I sit on the floor outside the door?"

"All right."

"Until you fall asleep."

"Okay," he said.

She sat cross-legged on the floor, leaning against the wall, and with nothing to do or nothing she wanted to think about, she began to count. Slowly, a count for each breath, she counted to three hundred and was sure he was asleep when he said, suddenly, "Mommy, I'm sorry to say, but I love you just a little tiny bit more than Dad. Just a tiny little bit more. Because sometimes I feel like I'm a little cute guy and Dad thinks no, you can't be a little cute guy, you're the big brother. But you let me be a little cute guy. That's why I love you a little tiny bit more than Dad."

"Mommies are very good at letting their little boys be little cute guys," Georgie said.

"I love you," he said.

"I love you, too."

"But don't leave yet, Mommy."

"I won't."

"Every time you leave I think I won't see Mommy again."

"Fergie," she said. "Mommy always comes back. Mommy always does."

She fell asleep on the floor and awoke later, after Fergus had finally fallen asleep. Feeling the cold, she went to our room and quickly put on her pajamas before crawling into bed. She burrowed against me in the dark, kissing me on the cheek. I stirred only slightly, and she said a small prayer into my shoulder.

We did not speak until morning, when her first words to me were, "It won't always be like this, Peter."

How every word she said then is now tinged by what I was soon to learn. She was talking about our lack of time together, apologizing for her busy schedule. Her birthday would be in a couple of weeks, her fortieth, and we hadn't even had time to talk about how she wanted to celebrate. It was a relief in a way to be so new in town, so that there was no question of a party. She had given me a splendid one for my fortieth, inviting forty friends who all contributed a song to a special CD she burned in secret and distributed to all the guests. There was no way I could have competed with that.

I asked her about it as I put on my tie. "You've got a birthday coming up," I said.

She burrowed deeper into the bed. "Don't remind me."

"What would you like to do?"

"Same as everyone. Time travel backwards. Nineteen eighty-nine would do nicely, I think."

"I'll work on it," I said. It was six-thirty in the morning, still dark. She lay in bed, eyes closed to the light I needed for dressing, half asleep and wanting to stay that way, because after I left at ten to seven, she would sleep another half-hour, until it was time to get the boys up and begin the morning ritual of feeding them breakfast, getting them dressed, finding their school bags, packing their homework and tracksuits and swimming gear, and getting them to school.

Though he loved his school uniform, Jack always put on his regular clothes first—backward—and Georgie had to get him changed. Fergus, who was generally up early, playing with his toys, would look up when she came in and ask, "Is it school today?" in such complete innocence that you could scarcely be mad at him, though Georgie always was. Liam was the hardest, fighting her every step of the way. His socks were too tight. His shirt felt crazy. His trousers were too wide. Even when she was herding them downstairs, chanting, "Shoes and coats! Shoes and coats!" Liam would still be searching for some excuse to run back up and find a different belt.

I leaned down to kiss her goodbye.

"It will get better," she said, reaching up and putting her warm hand against my cheek. "I don't know when it will, but it will."

"I'm not unaware that your work is exhausting," I said.

She nodded faintly against the pillow, but she was thinking,

Exhausting—no. *Exhilarating. Euphoric.* In a few hours she would be on her way to Dorset again, to the theater, to Mrs. Jordan, to him. What was exhausting for Georgie was coming back into her own life. Refereeing fights. Taking in the dry cleaning. Sweeping the kitchen floor after each and every meal. Getting them to put on those shoes every single morning.

A favourite part? Yes, of course, Miss Williams. All players have a favourite part, and mine has always been Rosalind.

I played Rosalind for twenty-seven years, first when I was pregnant with Dodee, and last just two years ago, when I was fifty-four years old. Rosalind, dear strong Rosalind. She knows what she loves and she gives her all to it. I do believe and solemnly swear to it that Rosalind has given me my finest moments on the stage.

I distinctly remember one evening, Miss Williams, when I played Rosalind in Bath. The theatre was greatly crowded there, and from the applause and admiration one would think that I had but started in the profession instead of being near the end of the race. With regard to acting, when I could for an hour or two forget everyone at Bushy and the various anxieties that in general depressed my spirits, I really thought, and it was the opinion of several critics there that had known me from my first appearance in London, that I was a better actress at that moment than I ever was. You would be surprised to see with what eagerness all the performers treasured up any little instruction I gave them at rehearsals; many of them made memorandums of them in their pocket books.

I drove the Duke and the children from my mind as much as I could during the time I was employed, but then they all returned with double force afterward, disturbing and confusing my dreams to a degree that was almost insupportable. I was forced to sit up in my bed half the night, feeling as if I should never see anyone at Bushy again. I wrote so to the Duke, and he wrote back that I was absurd for feeling so, but there was no cure for these agitated dreams.

*I*n her hotel room in Dorset he did not say, "I've been thinking of you all week."

She did not say, "What are we going to do?"

Neither of them called it a mistake.

They spoke instead of the evening's performance.

"You were magnificent," he said. "The audience loved you."

"I felt that. It's a shame Nicola didn't see it."

"Wish she were here, do you?"

"Not really."

They laughed.

"It feels like my show now," Georgie said. "Really. Well, except for the ending."

Her expectant look made him laugh again.

"You wouldn't tell Mr. Shakespeare to change something in one of his plays, would you?" he asked.

"*He* got it right."

"Don't get clever. I'm churlish because you're asking me to change what I've written. They're my words."

"They're her words."

"I've put them in her mouth."

"She put them on your paper. I'm going to keep after you." Her eyes—her eyes danced with the teasing.

"I can see that. You'll be happy to know I've been soliciting opinions on the ending. More so here than in London. These are real salt-of-the-earth types. I trust them completely."

"Even Thurrock of Whatsitwood?"

"Now, there you go. I didn't ask him."

"So what do these salt-of-the-earth types have to say about the ending?"

"Let's just say you're making some headway," he said.

"Glad to hear it."

"But the really fantastic news is Nicola's friend Richard swears he's coming to the show next weekend."

"Nicola said he was coming this weekend."

Piers shrugged. "Something came up. But he will come, and once he sees you, I know he'll want to take the show to the West End. He will love it, Georgie. He has to."

Piers's face suddenly became grave, the lines around his smiling eyes disappearing. "Lovely as the show was," he said, "I could barely stand to watch you. It was like staring at the sun."

He moved closer to her.

The proximity, was that all it was, the inching together of two bodies warm with the evening's triumph, the sense memory of being so close?

With no other words, they began to undress.

If they had to talk about it they would wait as long as they could. Talking things over was the realm of their real lives. This was something different. Georgie was in a railway hotel in the countryside, miles from London and husband and children, thousands of miles from where she really lived. In this place she performed under a roof seven centuries old, told the life story of a woman who was born two hundred years before she was, made love in a Tudor hotel with a man she barely knew.

To find this now, to have this man. There was something inestimable about it, something that flew in the face of love, guilt, moral duty. If the fortune was so good, it had to be accommodated.

She had missed for so many years the companionship of people like this, and now she felt her body recall what real life was like. It was to be back in wind and sun after a day in the cellar. The more she had, the more she found she needed.

*F*or a long time in my life I felt I knew everything there was to know about Georgie. Perhaps I know it still, but it's vestigial knowledge now, rotten or rotting. I have no use for it except in telling you this story.

Piers knew nothing about Georgie and I knew everything, but what did that matter if he was the one who had her?

I knew stupid things—that she would always choose the race car when playing Monopoly, the green marker in Sorry, heads first when we were flipping a coin. I knew she liked her salad with lemon juice, her coffee with milk but no sugar, her steak well-done. I knew she secretly loved country music ("the stories, the poor brokenhearted souls pining for their lost loves!"), despised jazz, preferred photographs to paintings but couldn't sit through a documentary.

I knew that she could not watch a young grandfather hoist a child onto his shoulders without a breathless longing for her own father, who had never once been able to do that for any of our sons.

And I also know that she would never have done what she did if her father were still alive.

Fergus Connolly adored his only daughter, and although his three sons were equally loved, he always made me feel like the son he never had. I became a part of his family's life, the big wreck of gatherings and ritual and drink, always the drink, right from the start, and though Georgie burst my bubble early on with her careless "Oh, he's like that with everyone," the patina of his regard stayed over me. Georgie's mother was ethereally there, painting in the other room or quietly pouring drinks, bringing in snacks—not put-upon, just independent. In fact, one of the most egalitarian marriages I had ever seen from that generation was Fergus and Pearl's.

But Pearl wasn't the one who drew me into the family, it was Fergus. Fergus, who smoked filterless cigarettes and drank two pints at the White Horse every afternoon after work for forty years of his life, Fergus, who said, *Every day above dirt's a blessing,* and *I want to be sick when I die.*

I will always remember Fergus on the day Georgie and I were married. We were supposed to make an early exit, off to begin the honeymoon, but we were having so much fun at the reception that we were among the last to leave.

"Take good care of my little girl," Fergus kept telling me.

My little girl. Georgie was thirty-four years old on our wedding day, I was thirty-six, and she was four months pregnant, but we felt younger than that—with our shabby futon and a couple of cartons of stuff, we certainly lived younger. We were kids to him—how could his little girl, his only girl, have gotten this old? We were married in the same church where he had married Pearl almost four decades before. He was sixty-eight years old and had retired the previous spring.

Fergus's eyes were on Georgie, dancing with her brother Tom, while next to her, her mother danced with Brendan, another brother.

Mother and daughter were nothing alike: Pearl was tiny and short-haired, birdlike, as I've said, and lovingly nicknamed Little Pearl by her sons, who treated her almost as some sort of mommy doll. Georgie was much taller, larger, with long frizzy hair and an outrageous laugh. It was almost impossible to see the mother in the daughter, but Fergus was studying them, looking back and forth between them, and I could tell that was exactly what he was seeing.

He held his beer to his chest and let his other arm swing straight out to the side.

The dregs of the wedding guests twirled around him, his wife and daughter and sons among them. He had been in this country more than forty years, married to Georgie's mother thirty-nine of them. Still, he shook his head.

"You know how much time there is between you and me?" he asked. He looked closely at my face as he held up his hand for me to see. His thumb and forefinger measured about an inch.

Four months later he was dead.

Her father's death—a heart attack, unexpected, coming just weeks before our own Fergus's birth—catapulted Georgie into a sphere she wasn't ready for, perhaps still isn't. I cannot say Georgie has ever gotten over it. Her relationship with her mother was not troubled, just never so close as with her dad, and though she loved her brothers, they were only brothers. Her father was her path-maker, the one who sent her on her way in the world, and when he was gone, perhaps she found it easier to falter.

She would never have done what she did if there had been even a chance he might have found out.

Georgie's fortieth birthday. She was in no way expecting me—we had celebrated the night before she left for Dorset, three days before her actual birthday. She let the boys choose the party and so we had dinner at Pizza Express, followed at home by a chocolate cake the boys helped Emma to make, homemade birthday decorations taped everywhere at waist level. Saturday was Georgie's birthday, and though she would be home Sunday morning, I decided to take the train down to Dorset to surprise her. I wanted to make a big romantic gesture, some sweeping statement of how much I loved her.

It's clear to me now that I could already feel her slipping away, though I must have felt it in the way you hear a siren on a busy city street, feeling the urgency but not knowing from which direction the sound is coming or whether you need to pull over.

Emma agreed to stay overnight with the boys, and so I took an afternoon train, hoping to catch her at the theater between the matinee and evening performances. I chose not to go to the matinee, because I knew she would be disconcerted if she heard my laugh or spotted me in the audience, as she surely would have. It would have made her anxious—*what had happened? why had I come? was there something wrong with the boys?*—and I didn't want to throw her performance off.

From the railway station, the taxi driver drove me out into the countryside, and when he drove down a dirt road to the barn, I was sure he had made a mistake.

"No," I said. "I mean the Tithe Barn *Theatre*." All I could see was an enormous stone barn that could not possibly serve such a sophisticated purpose.

"This is it, mate," the driver said.

Unconvinced, I got out of the taxi, leaving the door open and my overnight bag on the seat. "Would you mind waiting a minute?" I asked. "I just need to make sure I'm in the right place."

As I approached, the tithe barn seemed to me graceful yet somehow primitive, a structure nearly as old as the land on which it stood. Georgie had told me about it, but I hadn't, I realized, really listened. It was so huge, so medieval-looking. It barely looked man-made; it seemed a natural monolith rising straight from the core of the earth. I pulled open the heavy wooden door, expecting to see huge tractors or bales of hay, but instead I stepped into what clearly was a theater. To the right there was a small box office, to the left, a cozy sort of bar and refreshment stand, and in front of me a long, low table piled with programs. Beyond that was a cavernous open space, so dimly lit that I could see no stage or set.

There was a young woman behind the box-office desk, and I approached her, telling her who I was and asking for Georgie.

"Oh, they've all gone, I'm afraid," she said. "There's not much time between the matinee and the evening shows, and I'm sure they've just run out for a meal. But hang on, here's the director."

174

I turned around to catch Nicola passing me quickly, heading for the door.

"Hello," I said. "I'm Peter Martin. Georgie's husband?"

"Oh yes, of course," she said, holding out her hand. "Georgie didn't mention you were coming."

"It's a surprise," I said. "For her birthday."

"How lovely for her. She'll be so pleased. We did have it covered, though. Drinks after the show tonight with all the crew. We also have quite an important producer arriving later today."

"Georgie told me," I said. "Do you know where I could find her?" I asked.

"I'm fairly certain she went back to the hotel for a rest before tonight. I'm heading into town now. I would be more than happy to give you a lift."

"That's okay," I said. "I have a taxi waiting."

"All right, then," she said. "You know it's the Black Swan?"

I nodded.

"Georgie's in room twenty-six. Upstairs. They're notoriously understaffed at the front desk, so I doubt you'll find anyone to direct you. They give us an excellent rate, so we can't complain too much." Nicola smiled and resumed her pace, moving toward the door.

"This is some building, isn't it?" I said, walking with her but glancing back, trying to take in the building even as I was leaving it.

"That it is," Nicola said. "We love it."

"Well, thank you for your help," I said, as we parted just outside the barn. "I look forward to the show tonight."

"Fingers crossed that it's a good one," Nicola said. "To be honest, the pressure is on Georgie. If Richard Archibald takes a shine to the

175

show tonight we could be looking at *Shakespeare's Woman* on the West End."

"I know," I said. "Good luck."

Nicola crossed over to her car, and I had the taxi take me to the hotel, a Tudor building in the town center. Trapped between an equally ancient pub and a Boots, the hotel leaned slightly to the left, looking as if it would crumble to the ground immediately if either one of these buildings was suddenly removed. "Old-ie world-ie charm," Georgie had said.

I spied a florist down the road and dashed over to buy Georgie a dozen peach-colored roses.

Inside the small dark lobby there was no one around to ask, so I found my way through the rabbit warren of hallways and staircases to the second-floor room where Nicola had said Georgie was staying.

At first there was no answer to my knock, and if I were permitted to rewrite that moment of my life, there would never have been any answer. I would have turned and left the hotel; had a beer at a pub and then dinner; looked for Georgie after the show. But instead, I waited, listening, then knocked again, more loudly.

When she opened the door her eyebrows were raised in question, as if she expected me to be some member of staff—*Yes, may I help you, is there something you want?*

I put forth the roses I had brought.

"Peter," she said. Her eyebrows fell, the courteous smile collapsed. "I—I—I . . ." She threw herself against me as if we were in an automobile careening toward a tree and this was the only way to save me.

"It's okay," I said. "Nothing's happened. I—"

And then I saw him. In a scene that has forever spiraled through my mind, he sits on the dark wood of the recessed window ledge, looking not at me or at Georgie, but in a very cool, studied way, at the unmade bed.

No one rushed to explain that things weren't what they seemed. Georgie clung to me, trembling.

There was nothing to say and no one to say it. My hands had reflexively reached up to hold Georgie, but now I let them go limp by my sides. My overnight bag slipped from my shoulder, the roses fell to the floor.

Should I say that I was stunned? enraged? disbelieving? All those things, but mostly it was as if a grenade had blown my body to pieces and I had to, by sheer will, keep the pieces together, make the body whole enough to walk across the room.

"What have you done?" I whispered hoarsely. "What have you done?"

I wanted to put my hands around her neck. Instead, I went for him.

"Look," he said, standing up. "This is not good. But let's be sensible."

The fight started there, by the window where he was, and moved across the room toward Georgie.

"You bastard, you fucking bastard, you fucking bastard," I said. I pummeled him with my fists while Georgie screamed at me to stop. I wouldn't stop, I couldn't. He deflected my blows expertly. He knew what he was doing. I kept going for him, his face and neck. He hit me hard in the stomach. I thought I would kill him, I could think of nothing but killing him. The taste in my mouth was of metal and rotten meat, the taste of rage.

When he saw the chance, he pushed past me toward the door.

"I'll just go," he said. "Georgie, if you're okay?"

Georgie, standing at the center of the room, palms upturned, crying, could do no more than weakly nod. I was leaning against a table, breathing heavily. Piers paused at the doorway, seeming to take in the entire scene.

He was a playwright; he probably appreciated the staging.

"Thirty minutes, Georgie," he said quietly. He was talking about the curtain.

I lunged and kicked at the door as it closed behind him. I wanted to hit him again, I wanted to hit her. These urges assailed me like nausea, and I balled my fists tighter, pressed them into my sides.

Georgie's eyes were wide and frightened, focused on me. "I can't believe this," she said. "I can't believe this is happening." She came toward me.

"Don't touch me," I barked, as frightened of myself as she was.

Her face was contorted, her cheeks pink and growing pinker. She had her head covered in pin curls held in place by a hundred bobby pins, and she wore a blue striped shirt I didn't recognize, a wrinkled and oversized man's shirt—

His shirt.

"It's over this second," Georgie said. "Right now. It won't ever happen again. I promise you that. Oh, Peter." Her voice cracked. "I'm so sorry."

She had finally stopped trying to touch me and instead just stood in the middle of the room with her monstrous screwed-up face, shiny with mucus and tears.

"How long?" I asked.

"Just since Dorset," she said. "Not in London at all. Just these past three weekends."

Three weekends.

In the space of a lifetime, what were three weekends?

Could they be erased, rectified in some way, or were they enough to forever alter the outcome of several lives?

"I didn't mean for this to happen," Georgie said. "You believe me, don't you?"

"Do I *believe* you?" I asked. "What the hell do you think?" I was shaking, grasping my shoulders with my hands to try to stop.

Later, I would want to know every detail, every single moment of what had passed between them, but for now I wanted only for time to go backward so that I could miss the train or decide not to come at all, never then having to find out.

The disgust I felt for wanting that, of all things, for craving simple feeble ignorance. Because I didn't want to do what I had to do—push back against her, punish her, hurt her and hurt her and hurt her back. I wanted instead never to have known.

"You're coming with me," I said.

"Oh, Peter," she said. "Thank you." *Thank you*—as if it were over, as if I had already forgiven her for what I hadn't yet begun to comprehend she had done.

"Now," I said.

"Yes," she said. "Of course. Tonight."

"Now."

The relief began to turn. "There's no understudy," she said slowly. "I have to do the show. But afterwards—"

"Cancel it," I said.

"I can't. Please understand. Please. It's just two hours. Just until after the show. Wait for me. There's this producer coming, remember, this West End guy. We've got to do—"

"Fuck you," I said, and walked out of the room.

I had said, *Now—if you hold out any hope at all, come right now—* and she had said, *This producer—*

And I knew. I knew: If she didn't come with me then, if she chose to stay and play her part instead, any return she would eventually muster would not be permanent, and would not be for me.

It's possible that all that needed to pass between the two of us did so there, in that hotel room.

If only I had left it at that.

Please go for my letters, Miss Sketchley.

You already have and there was nothing?

Well, then, you must go again.

I suppose you want to know about that letter, Miss Williams, the one I received in Cheltenham. That is a letter the world would have liked to read.

I was playing Nell in Devil to Pay *the afternoon the Duke's letter arrived. He wrote to inform me that he wanted me to meet him at Maidenhead the following day to discuss the terms of . . . a separation.*

Miss Williams, his letter gave no reason for this. My head confused and my hand unsteady, I sat down to reply:

"Yes, I will come but must exert myself, play and farce tonight. I will be in Maidenhead by three on Saturday. As I remain, Your Royal Highness, your faithful servant."

His faithful servant. For twenty years I was his dear Dora, his beloved Dora, and now it seemed I was to be his faithful servant and he My Royal Highness.

I arrived at the theatre dreadfully weakened by a succession of fainting fits. When Jobson, playing the cobbler, was meant to accuse the conjurer of making me "laughing drunk," I tried to laugh but cried instead and poor Jobson was forced to improvise. "Why, Nell," he said, "the conjurer has made thee crying drunk."

After the performance I did not even get out of my costume before boarding a chaise and traveling all night to meet the Duke.

I was heartsick, but my spirits were for a moment relieved when I saw his dear familiar face. He took my hands in his and he told me, "You have been the most excellent of women, Mrs Jordan."

But in almost the same breath he told me we were to separate. He promised to make generous provisions for his children and for me; his lawyers would draw up papers outlining my allowance.

Why?

Why, you ask?

The Duke had fallen in love with Miss Tynley Long, a young beauty he had met at a fête at Carlton House. It was not her beauty alone that enchanted the Duke. She was an heiress, you see, and the Duke was at that time in terrible danger of not covering his debts. I could no longer earn enough to be of greatest assistance, and the Regent did nothing to help relieve this financial embarrassment. It had become increasingly necessary for the Duke to marry, and he was greatly pressured by the queen to find someone suitable under the Royal Marriage Act. Miss Tynley Long was suitable, you see, while I was not.

And though we had never had for twenty years the semblance of a quarrel, I had to submit to his word.

A separation.

He held my face in his hands and bid me goodbye. Twenty years, Miss Williams, twenty years and ten children together, and after that afternoon in Maidenhead I was never to meet the Duke again.

Mrs. Jordan went on the day her world began to fall apart, and Georgie did the same. This character, the stage—they were like drugs to her. As everything began to slip out of her grasp, Mrs. Jordan took over and saved her for an hour and a half.

Georgie felt closer to Mrs. Jordan than she ever had; her performance reached beyond script and staging and props to make fluid any boundaries between actor and character that may have still remained. She was on the edge of tears throughout, the edge of tears like the edge of orgasm—frantic, feral, exigent, the center of the universe and the only place anyone wants to look.

They loved her that night. Gave her a standing ovation. She wanted only for the audience to leave, but they wouldn't let her go, holding her in their gaze, keeping her right where they wanted her— just there, in front of them, playing her role.

She left the stage finally, with relief, exhausted, and went to her dressing room, but the relief faded as she began to take off her makeup. She was alone, I was gone, and in the mirror was the face of the stranger who had betrayed me.

And then she longed to be Mrs. Jordan again, to be anyone at all but the woman who had to play this role, live this life.

She ignored the knock that came a few minutes later, but Nicola eased open the door anyway.

"Good God, Georgie, what's happened?" she asked.

"I've got to go home," Georgie said. "Now. Tonight."

"I'm so sorry. I saw your husband earlier. Is there an emergency at home?"

Georgie put her head down on her hands on the makeup table and wept into the bend in her arm.

"Can I help at all?" Nicola asked.

"I need to get back," Georgie said.

"Right," Nicola said briskly. "I don't think there are any more trains tonight. I'm fairly certain the last one was at half-eight. But let me get Piers. We'll see what we can organize."

"No," Georgie said, raising her head slightly, "wait," but Piers appeared even before Nicola could go to look for him.

He entered the dressing room and placed his hands lightly on her shoulders.

"Listen," he said, "I know the timing is terrible, but I've been speaking with Nicola's friend Richard and he wants to go out for drinks to discuss—"

"No," Georgie said.

"I made the mistake—before—of telling him it was your birthday and he's keen to . . ." He was trying to talk to her reflection in the mirror, but she refused to meet his eyes.

"Piers, for God's sake," Nicola said. "What is wrong with you? Look at her."

"No," Georgie said, through clenched teeth. "I did the show. I did the goddamned show." *Which may have cost me my marriage,* she did not add. Slowly, Nicola's face seemed to deepen in understanding.

"Sorry," Piers said, and the absence of the *I'm,* the extreme stinginess of that missing pronoun, told Georgie how little this, how little *she,* meant to him. Her heart began to beat furiously. She would find a way to make him the villain in all this.

"I need to get home tonight," Georgie said. "Where can I rent a car?"

"Here?" Piers said. "I can't imagine where you could do that."

"She can't drive in this state, Piers." Nicola asked. "Isn't there anything you can do?" She looked at him sharply.

It took a number of moments, but he finally offered, "I could certainly drive you back."

"Well, then," Nicola said.

Georgie didn't decline his offer. She wanted to get back, she had to get back, and this appeared the only way.

Nicola was kind, and helped Georgie gather her things, leading her away by the arm like an invalid. Who would have expected Nicola to be such a human being? Perhaps she had done this more than once before, picked up the pieces of Piers's romances. Perhaps not long ago someone had done it for her.

When it came time to leave, I don't know if Georgie paused at the door of the tithe barn, if she turned to look back at those centuries-old walls and roof timbers, but I have her pausing there, sensing somehow, as I did when I thought about it later, all that she was leaving behind. These medieval walls now held this thing we had called our marriage, not just the detritus, but the goodness of it as well, all I had given to her and she to me in the twelve years we were together. This cavernous space, one hundred forty feet long, thirty-four feet wide, forty feet high, was not possibly big enough to store all that had passed between us, and yet now it did, everything from our life together, all the way back to the beginning, when we were two people who moved in together within days of meeting; when she was someone who whispered "I love you" under her breath as we stood at the altar reciting our formal wedding vows; when I was the man crying about how perfect those little boys were when they slipped out of Georgie's body and landed in my arms. All of this would be locked away in the tithe barn, which became for me now not just the place where my marriage ended but, true to its original purpose, a storehouse—a storehouse for all of our years together, almost a third of my life, fully half of my heart, and everything I had ever given—lovingly, willingly—to her.

*T*he drive back to London was long and slow and mostly silent. Georgie sat with her knees drawn up against the glove box, trying not to cry. There was very little for her to say to Piers. Their affair had barely started and she was already intent on ending it. When he asked, "Is there anything I can do to help the situation?" Georgie gave him a look of disbelief.

"What do you think?" she said. "You're an undomesticated creature, Piers. I can imagine all you want to do is flee from this scene."

"You're nothing to flee from," Piers said.

"Oh, yeah? You fled quickly enough when my husband arrived."

"I thought it was for the best," Piers said. "Did you expect me to stay and defend your honor?"

It was all she could do to keep herself from asking him to pull over, turn around, do anything but take her home. She felt as if she were being summoned to a deathbed—needing to rush home, yet not wanting to face what she had to when she got there. They carried on mostly in silence, but it became one more thing to devastate me, this little road trip, taking on epic proportions as I envisioned them alone for hours, driving peacefully and safely back to London late at night,

Radio 4 voices discussing health-care concerns and the latest military biographies in hushed, sane tones.

It was three a.m. when they reached our house. Like a teenager who didn't want to shine the headlights into her parents' bedroom window, Georgie asked Piers to let her out at the end of the street.

"Is this goodbye?" he asked her.

"This is goodbye," she said.

"I don't envy you the rest of this night," he said, and she vaguely felt he was telling her he'd been through this sort of thing innumerable times before.

He got out of the car to hand her her bag and then went to take her in his arms.

"No," she said. "I can't." But how she wanted in a way to deposit herself into his quiet, unencumbered life instead of facing the mess she'd made of hers.

"Ring me if you need me," he said. "I'll wait until you're safely inside." He sat in his car at the end of the road like a London taxi driver, making sure she was all right before driving away.

She unlocked the door, but the chain was on. Had I locked her out? she wondered, but after a long ring of the doorbell Emma appeared, dazed and a little frightened.

"Where's Peter?" Georgie asked her.

"No." Emma sounded confused. "He went to see you in the, in the . . ."

"The play. He hasn't come back yet?"

"No. Has something happened?"

"A misunderstanding. Are the boys okay?"

"Sleeping. Is everything all right, Georgie? You gave me a fright."

"You haven't heard from him?" Georgie asked.

"No, I haven't."

"Okay, Emma, it's okay. Just go back to bed."

"Are you sure, Georgie?"

Emma retreated uncertainly to the sofa bed in the sitting room, and Georgie fought the urge to tell her everything. It would have been very like Georgie to do that, to unload on whoever happened to be there, but she resisted, childishly thinking that if she didn't tell anyone it couldn't possibly be true.

Leaving Emma, Georgie rushed upstairs to look at her sleeping sons. She opened the door quietly but couldn't help herself from going into the room. Jack still slept like a baby with his arms spread perpendicular to his body. She picked up his small hand and brought it to her lips. Fergus was curled around his stuffed doggie, and Liam slept with his eyes open just far enough to seem as if he saw everything in his sleep. She looked at them for a long time and even then couldn't bear to leave them, so she took a pillow and blanket from our bed and went to sleep on the top floor landing, just outside their room.

Not long after, before she could fall asleep, Fergus called out to her. She went to him immediately. He was sitting up in his bed, but when he saw her he lay back with relief against the pillow.

"What's the matter, sweet peach?" she asked.

"I need to ask you something, Mommy," he said, showing no surprise that she should be there. "It's true you can't get back into your dream when you wake up, right?"

"Did you have a bad dream, sweetheart?"

"No, I had a very good dream. I dreamed I was about to eat some lovely chicken nuggets, and then I woke up. I would really like to be back in that dream with those chicken nuggets."

"Maybe we can get you back there," she said. She sprinkled kisses on his head—seeds for good dreams—and made a pitcher from her hand to water them.

"These are for more chicken nugget dreams," she said.

"Thank you, Mom. I just needed to ask you that."

Instead of returning to her spot on the landing, she pulled the blanket and pillow into the boys' room, staying the rest of the night on the floor next to Fergus's bed, crying into the pillow so he wouldn't hear.

I didn't go home for three days.

I reached London just as the pubs were about to close but found a small tourist hotel near Waterloo station with a lobby bar that stayed open late. I had drunk a few beers already, on the train, and now I sat on a barstool, blinking at myself in the mirror, watching myself drink more.

The bar was almost empty. A beautiful young Middle Eastern couple sat quietly holding hands at a table in the corner, and in the center of the room were three American women in their twenties, drunk and a little loud. The bartender was chatty with the others but didn't say much to me until he announced, "Last orders, mate." When I didn't budge he nodded at my overnight bag and asked, "Need some help up to your room?"

"No," I muttered, but the idea was planted and I stumbled with my bag to the front desk, where the clerk took one look at me and handed me a key.

Upstairs in the hotel room, alone for the first time since leaving Dorset, I threw myself on the bed and turned on the TV—the pitiful BBC, supplemented by a few cable stations the hotel offered, nothing like the hundreds of channels that could have numbed my mind in the U.S. I flipped between a gardening show, a documentary on airports, and a nature program about pandas. They are always inches away from starvation, it seems, and have to eat virtually all the time to get enough calories to keep themselves alive.

I had bought a pack of cigarettes at the train station—my first in maybe ten years—and smoked one after another.

I was drunk, I was more than drunk, and the minute I took my attention off of the pandas on TV, I began to cry.

"You bitch!" I said out loud. "You whore"—and worse. There was no one to hear me. I writhed in the bed, fitful and sweaty, as if in a ship's cabin on a choppy sea. I cried for hours, it felt like, the way you can only cry in a hotel room with the TV on loud and no one you know on the other side of the wall to keep quiet for. I cried so much I felt like I was dying, and when I stopped I felt strangely, briefly healed, as if it were morning and everything was all right, a feeling that lasted only seconds before evaporating again into despair.

For maybe the first time in my life I understood the meaning of drinking to kill the pain. It was a real physical pain, searing and inescapable. Implanted in my brain was an image of Georgie with him, in bed, with him, in bed, with him, in bed, and I craved what would dull it. Drink. Unconsciousness. Getting the hell out.

Toward dawn I must have passed out, because I awoke to sunlight, sweat-soaked in my T-shirt and underwear, reeking of nicotine and gripped by terror and the fierce single-mindedness of a hangover. I got up and closed the blinds. It was past noon, almost twenty-four hours since I'd eaten anything. The hotel was too small to have room service, and there was no way I could have made it to the lobby, let alone out onto the street. I flipped through the telephone book, trying to find a pizza place that would deliver. My hands shook violently, my head spun, and I had to lie down twice before making the call.

It took over an hour for the pizza to come. I had ordered a big bottle of Coke, too, and three beers. Beer doesn't come in six-packs in England, and I thought three a judicious number. Enough to take the edge off but not enough to send me back toward drunkenness.

I rummaged around in my bag for some aspirin and came across a card Fergus had tucked into it just before I left. *Happy Brithday Mommy*, it said, with a picture of Georgie drawn on the cover and inside two stick figures, one tall and one short, which I took to be Fergus and me. The twins were nowhere to be seen. Fergus had commanded me to give Georgie the card the minute I saw her. I lay back on the bed and turned it over to read another message on the back: *You have bee a good mommy.*

In the artificially darkened room my trembling fingers explored the waxy crayon words on thick, pulpy construction paper.

"Damn you," I whispered, reaching for the lighter that was on the bedside table, next to the cigarettes. I lit the card on fire and watched it slowly burn. When the flames reached my hands, I blew them out.

Betrayal clawed through my chest from under my skin. I felt abandoned there in the hotel room, irrationally seizing on the fact that Georgie had not come after me, though there was no possible way she could have known where I was. Unbelievably, I was not thinking yet of leaving her, of kicking her out, of taking the kids and running away. It seemed still that a horrible calamity had happened to all of us, a meteor crashing into our lives and blowing everything to bits. I had not managed to learn, either from Shakespeare or from life, that as long as we can say, "This is the worst," we have not yet met the worst.

I didn't leave the room at all that day, never really moving from the bed or turning off the TV as the afternoon turned to evening and then to night. I smoked cigarette after cigarette and drank the three beers, finished the pizza that had been sitting in the room for hours.

On Monday morning I called in sick to work, telling them I had the stomach flu so they wouldn't ask too many questions. When I turned my phone on I saw there were many messages from Georgie, but I didn't listen to them and quickly turned the phone back off before she tried to ring me again.

Around lunchtime I managed a shower and finally left the hotel, just to go for a walk. I have always been cheered by crowds, not the kinds that gather in one place for a single purpose—huge festivals or concerts or sporting events—but the kinds that move naturally through city streets, with their purposeful strides, knocking into you with gentle carelessness while their attention is focused elsewhere. Strangers on the street, other people's conversations in the café where I stopped to eat—these things calmed me, brought me slightly back into the world. Some windowpane onto rationality appeared, at least for a while, and though I was calmer, I was far, far sadder.

I guess it would have made sense, as I walked around southeast London, so close to home I could have crossed one of the bridges and walked there in less than an hour, to decide what to do. But that was impossible. A meteor crashes into your house, there are no decisions to make. All you can do is go through the rubble.

I found myself doing something I used to do as a kid: I picked a face from the crowd, a face remarkable neither for its beauty nor ugliness, a face almost ordinary in appearance, and tried to memorize it. I would stare and stare, cataloguing each feature so that (my kid self thought) if called upon to give a description—say, if moments later the person committed a crime—I would be able to identify him in a lineup. Yet no matter how hard I tried, I could never, even an hour or so later, bring a picture of this person's face to my mind. I could sometimes recite the phrases I had used to describe his features to myself—*thinning brown hair, large gold glasses*—but never would a face in its entirety appear to me. I had always wondered if this was a particular visual inadequacy of mine or if it was part of the brain's natural design. I had read once that Leonardo da Vinci would spend an entire day following a stranger with an interesting face and then go home and paint the face from memory. But I always failed to recall the face I had selected, and today the only face I could bring to my mind was my wife's.

I was unable even to picture Piers, and that seemed to unjustly make me the victim of a crime for which the criminal had not been caught. I had only seen him twice in my life. He was no less a stranger to me than any of these people I passed on the street, and that fact more than anything seemed to me the cruelest measure of how removed I was from the life I thought I had been living.

In late afternoon I bought a bottle of wine and some food and came back to the hotel, my new sanctuary. I spent one more night there and part of another day, but by Tuesday afternoon I was missing my sons too much. I had no speech planned for Georgie, but I wanted to hold my little boys, hug them and talk to them, so I paid the hotel bill, got on the tube, and made the fifteen-minute journey home.

*T*urning the corner into our little street, I had the feeling I had been gone a very, very long time. The buds on the cherry trees had blossomed wildly in the past few days, and the wonderful pinkness of the trees against the pretty pastel houses made the street look like a movie set. It was too perfectly perfect to be real. Our little pink house embodied the architectural style any child in the Western world would have drawn if you asked him for a picture of "a house."

Georgie appeared at the window as I approached, as if she had been standing there, Penelope-like, the entire time I had been gone. The door opened and she came out onto the sidewalk.

"I heard your footsteps," she said. "I've been worried sick." She moved toward me for an embrace, and I held up my hand to keep her away.

"I didn't know if you were coming back," she said.

"I think you know me better than that," I said.

"I made dinner," she said, flashing me a wincing, apologetic sort of smile. Georgie, who never made dinner, had made dinner. "Veal piccata."

Then the stampede began, down the stairs and directly into my arms, all three boys squealing my name. I held their small bodies against me, smelled their hair, kissed their necks.

"You had workin', Dad?" Liam asked.

"Yes," I said. "I had working."

For a brief moment I was a returning war hero, and they fought for my arms and attention, then just as quickly lost interest, wanting to get back to their game.

"We're playing last kitty in the pet shop," Jack said. "Want to play with us, Dad?"

Why had we had these children? What did we possibly think we could offer these gorgeous, trusting souls, these three little heartbeats that together we had created from nothing?

If it were just Georgie and me, everything would have been so easy. I would have walked out. I would have drunk too much, slept around, been a little cruel for a few months, a little stupid. I would have slowly, painfully started to get over her. I could have behaved like a man. But now I was a father, and being a father made you less of a man, I could see. It left you powerless to do what you really wanted to do, because you had these children, you loved these children, you needed them and they needed you. I could almost bring myself to despise Georgie for making me a father as much as I did for her infidelity.

❧

After veal piccata and homework, baths and books, we put the boys to bed. Bedtime rituals are designed to give children comfort and a kind of routine, but tonight they were for me. The familiarity kept me sane, and afterward I went to sit in the chair in the sitting room and Georgie came in and curled at my feet on the floor.

"Peter," she said.

I stared into the glass of red wine I had poured for myself.

"If you only knew how sorry I am," she said.

"It's not about sorry," I said slowly. "It's about why you did it."

"Would you please look at me?"

"I can't," I said. "I can't look at you."

"If you would look at me you would see how little it meant. It was stupid. I was just caught up in the play, it just happened. It was the worst mistake I ever made."

"If it was stupid you wouldn't have done it," I said, my voice a wine-soaked monotone. "You don't do stupid things."

"I did. I did this."

"I hope it was worth it."

"Don't say that," she said quickly.

"Are you in love with him?" I asked

"No! God, no, nothing like that. Nothing. There's nothing. I—"

"Stop saying 'nothing,'" I said. "It was something. It was a hell of a lot."

"I don't know why it happened, but I swear to you it's over.

"If you don't even know why it happened, how can you be so sure it's over?"

"It is, I swear to you."

"Why now?" I asked. "Why not in New Jersey, when you were miserable and you hated your fucking life. Ever since we came to London, you can't stop talking about how *happy* you are, how *perfect* your life is, how *everything* has changed. 'Thank you, Peter, for bringing me here.' And I bought it. 'Thank you for letting me suck some other guy's cock so I can feel truly fulfilled.'"

"Stop it," she said, wincing. "Please. It's nothing like that."

"If you say 'nothing' one more time I am going to smash your skull in with this bottle." Was I really threatening her? Could she ever come to be afraid of me?

She was quiet for a moment and then said, "I love you, Peter. I love our family."

"Clearly," I said.

"It won't happen again. I told you that, it's over. I'll never see him again, I promise, except for the show—"

"'Except for the show,'" I mimicked cruelly. "Everything on your terms." She was at my feet—had she calculated that submissive pose to make me feel I had authority when I really was the one without any? I grew acutely suspicious of the actress in her, the actress the woman might use when she needed to.

"I know it's going to be really hard," she said, making it sound like I was facing a difficult round of exams, some challenging athletic competition, "But we can get through this, Peter. We'll get some counseling, we'll—"

"I don't want to talk anymore," I said abruptly.

"We have to talk. We—"

"Don't tell me what we have to do," I said.

I stood up, stepping around her there on the floor in order to leave the room and go upstairs. If she had touched me, like some horror-film villain grabbing your ankle after you think he's dead, I swear I would have kicked her in the ribs.

My second night home was worse than the first. Georgie was going back down to Dorset the next day for another round of performances, and it all seemed so final, as if she was going off to war and this was our only chance.

I poured myself a scotch and she told me everything—when she sucked his cock, how many times he went down on her, whether they fell asleep together and if so whether they were in each other's arms. I asked her for every detail—that's what I thought I wanted—and she gave me all.

My sarcastic questions, her tender and soothing replies, terrible scenes, tears, one of us crumpling on the floor, the other holding on, a door slammed, someone hiding in the bathroom with a lapful of balled-up Kleenex, crying inconsolably. We confined it to the kitchen, this violent, churning activity, keeping it deep underground to prevent it from rising up through the house and consuming the boys as they slept.

But there was nowhere to go with any of it. All I could do was ask the same questions over and over again. Why now, I asked. Why not in New Jersey when you were miserable? Or *do you love him? Do you love* him? DO YOU LOVE HIM? a hundred times.

No, she always said vehemently, denying love, denying everything I accused her of except what she could not deny. "A mistake," she called it. "That's all it was."

A mistake.

All.

"You're going to have to find some other rhetoric," I croaked at her. "'A mistake'? Oops—I left the muffins in the oven too long. Oops—by accident, I fucked somebody's brains out on eight separate occasions."

"Peter—"

"Jesus Christ, Georgie, don't you see what you've done to me?"

I humiliated myself again by crying, and she cried, too, trying to hold me, comfort me. We were like two newborn, sightless animals, groping at each other, trying to find our places in the world.

"You have no idea what you've done," I said, turning abruptly from her.

I felt hypnotized by an image of Georgie on the floor with Piers, naked, calling his name. I held on to that image until I could just about bear it, lull myself into thinking that like a soldier in battle watching men die again and again, I had become used to it. But then I swiveled in my chair to get up for a drink and there was another image there to deliver its physical blow and I began to shake and weep again, feeling no different than I had when I had first discovered her in the hotel room.

She said, "I'm sorry, Peter. I guess I was so consumed by my new life I lost sight of you. Of my old life. And that's my fault, too."

"So now I'm part of your old life?"

"Of what's important, I mean. You, the boys."

"Oh, come off it. Maybe it wasn't New Jersey you hated. Maybe it was me."

"That's not true."

"What exactly *is* true? Here's this guy, this *writer*, Georgie, for God's sake. Did I disappoint you so much . . ." I felt myself starting to shake.

"It's over," Georgie said. "If I could undo it I would. Already it seems like it wasn't even real."

"Wasn't real? Wasn't real?" I willed myself not to break down, changed my course from tears toward rage, and suddenly I had my hands on her. I was shaking her, my fingers digging into her shoulders while her head lurched back and forth. "To you, to you it wasn't

real. Look at me, I'm a fucking mess. How can you say it wasn't real?
It was *real*. It *was* real."

"Daddy, Mommy," I heard.

I took my hands off Georgie and held them, fingers flexed, in front
of me. When I turned toward the bottom of the stairs, Jack stood
there, clutching his stuffed pony and rubbing his eyes.

"I was calling and calling you," he said indignantly, and for a moment I thought he hadn't seen what happened.

"I'm sorry, sweetie," Georgie said brightly. "We didn't hear you."
She scooped him up in her arms, and he clung to her neck, burying
his face in her hair.

"You're not allowed to hurt Mommy," he said, his voice muffled
against Georgie's skin.

"I didn't," I said. And then, "I mean, I know."

Georgie carried our son back upstairs. Had it been Liam, he would
have come at me swinging, ready to take on any sort of monster who
might threaten his mother. Jack was terrified, needed comforting. Oh
God, I thought, would he carry this picture with him for the rest of
his life?

I sat at the table with my head in my hands. I thought I would sit
there alone for hours, feeling the sticky circle of juice on the tabletop
against my cheek, my head buried in shame, but after about twenty
minutes, Georgie came back and sat at the table across from me.

I sat up and looked at her. She reached out and took my hand.

"I'm sorry," I said.

"I won't let you hurt me, Peter."

"I won't," I said.

"You've had too much to drink," she said.

I was silent. It was an old argument. Her father and brothers had drunk too much, she thought, and whenever I appeared poised to follow in their footsteps, she would speak up. For her to bring this up now aroused in me all the anger that had been briefly doused by shame.

We sat in silence for some time, and I felt not one shred of hope materialize between us. It is difficult to explain. All I can say is that when I looked at Georgie I saw two different people, the one I loved and the one who had broken my heart, and I had no idea how to dispose of one without also losing the other. I felt like someone contemplating suicide, desperately wanting to live yet knowing the only way to end his pain was to end his life.

"Peter," she said. "I'm begging you."

For forgiveness. That's what she needed from me—now, or later (she would wait). It was the only thing she required and the only thing, it turned out, I couldn't provide.

It was as simple as that. Even when those I loved most depended on my forgiveness, I could not find a way to manufacture it.

I would never have expected myself to be so incapable of forgiveness. I was raised on turning the other cheek—a staple for those of us on the fringes of the Bible Belt, a necessary character trait in the Midwest. I had spent a large part of my life forgiving everyone— my family and friends for their faults, strangers for any unkindnesses, the world for not being perfect, myself for failing to become the man I had always planned to be. I was so good at cutting everyone slack, at bending and bending to accommodate others, and especially her. I was now convinced that if I bent once more I would break forever.

I didn't want to be a broken man.

Maybe it was simply the unwavering faith she had that I *would* forgive her that made me so incapable of doing it. Who's to say whether I was wrong or right, whether I should have tried harder, given it more time. Wrong or right doesn't matter when the story becomes about what you're capable of doing and what, through no lack of trying, you aren't.

We were both exhausted from not knowing from one minute to the next what we were going to say or do. My head felt cloudy with the alcohol I had not been without since I found her with Piers. I didn't know what to say to her. I didn't know what to do. I fished around in my pocket for my cigarettes and laid them on the table while I searched for a lighter.

"You're smoking again, too?" Georgie asked.

I felt the rage rising in me again, the now familiar urge to put my hands around her neck. I was glad she was leaving.

"Don't come back," I choked out.

"What?"

"When you go to Dorset I don't want you to come back."

"Oh, come on, Peter." Her look, more disbelieving than shocked, gave me further fuel. I groped for words. I was trying this out; how did this work? How did a man go about kicking his wife out of his house, especially when he wasn't at all sure that was what he wanted to do?

"I can't . . ." I said. "I need you to . . ." I struggled with the gravelly knot of revulsion in my throat. "Just stay," I said. "Just stay for the rest of the show. I need you to be gone."

"Don't. Peter, don't," Georgie said. "You can't."

"I can," I said, suddenly practical. "It's a company lease. My name is on it, not yours. I'll have the locks changed."

"No," she said. "These are my children, this is my home. I'm not staying away."

"Yes," I said. Even I could hear the menace in my voice. "Yes, you are."

My spirits were so depressed, and I was convinced that money, money, or the want of it, had made the Duke the most wretched of men, but having done wrong he did not like to retract. Miss Sketchley was at Bushy occasionally and she said the Duke was thin and by no means in spirits. I don't wonder at this. With all his excellent qualities, his domestic virtues, his love for his lovely children, what might he not have suffered?

You say I am perhaps too generous to the Duke, Miss Williams? I believe I hear in your statement that you think me a fool. But I will not hear the Duke abused. He did wrong and he suffered for it. I ask you, Miss Williams, what will not a woman do who is firmly and sincerely attached? Had he left me to starve, I would never have uttered a word to his disadvantage.

But the press thought as you do, Miss Williams. My friend Peter Pindar wrote:

What! leave a woman to her tears?
Your faithful friend for twenty years;
One who gave up her youthful charms,
The fond companion of your arms!

Brought you ten smiling girls and boys,
Sweet pledges of connubial joys,
As much your wife in honor's eye,
As if fast bound in wedlock's tie.

Return to Mistress Jordan's arm,
Soothe her, and quiet her alarms,
Your present differences o'er,
Be wise, and play the fool no more.

For months, everyone awaited the Duke's return, but return he did not. As it happened, Miss Tynley Long would not have the Duke. All women were not to be taken by an open attack, it seemed, and a premeditated one stood a worse chance than any other. And so it was that the Duke remained alone while I was forced to quit Bushy forever. Through his lawyers and advisors, he urged me to find cheap and convenient accommodation in London, and I took a house on Cadogan Place. The children would be permitted to stay with me until they were thirteen, but as the boys go to school at seven anyway, Tuss was my only boy, and then only for a few months. As for the girls, Sophy was already sixteen and so charming in mind and person that she regularly accompanied the Duke to parties and was now accustomed to receiving his friends at Bushy. She must remain with him, as that provided her with her best chance.

I was delighted to have the younger girls, but then I began to worry that if they remained with me they would grow out of the Duke's heart, and the less the Duke saw them the less he would care for them. What a royal father may offer his children is so much greater than what a mother in my position could do, and so I finally determined that they must all leave me to stay under the Duke's roof and protection. They would come to me often for visits, they would remain near to me always, but they must live with him.

I can see you do not understand, Miss Williams, but I tell you it had to be this way. Giving the children up would have been death to me if I were not so strongly impressed with the certainty of it being for their future advantage.

She called me as soon as the show finished that first evening back in Dorset, as if to prove she was alone in her room at the Black Swan, being good, doing her penance.

"It's a true one-woman show now," she said, taking a stab at cheerfulness. "Nicola came for tonight's performance, but she went back to London right afterward. This is so end-of-run for her. She's already on to her next play. I'm basically on my own with the crew." No mention of Piers. They had agreed he would stay away for the duration of the show—at least that's what she told me.

After a short silence she blurted out, "I wish you had come."

"What?"

"All of you, I mean—come with me. Taken some time off. The boys could use a break from school," she added unconvincingly.

"You want me to come on a little vacation with you?" I heard myself asking.

"Just to spend some time together, Peter."

"I imagine you would be lonely without your lover there."

I loathed the way we spoke to each other, I to her with a fetid mixture of sarcasm and self-pity, and she to me with gentle solicitousness, as if cajoling some child to take a chance on the wide, wide world out there.

Pathetic as our conversations were, I couldn't *not* talk to her. We both had this urgent desire to stay on the phone, terrified that if we hung up any semblance of hope for our family would vanish. I had felt this way before—not with Georgie, but with my first girlfriend, Karen, my hometown honey. After I went away to college, I would come back from the library at night or the campus bars and call her. We would stay on the phone for hours, even when neither one of us could come up with a word to say. Karen was washing hair at a beauty salon in Aledo, Illinois, and I was encountering Plato and Nietzsche for the first time at Northwestern University, but letting her go felt like an act of disloyalty to my entire past. And so I kept calling, and our relationship, like those phone calls, dragged on far longer than it should have.

When it seemed Georgie and I were both about to fall asleep on the phone, we slipped away without really saying goodbye. Phone on my chest, I dozed in the chair and then lurched awake. Georgie! The pain was still there, still needing killing, and I went downstairs for some wine and then up to my room, where I turned on the little bedroom TV and wondered if this was the sad sum total of what my life would be from now on: being hit again and again with what she had done, to come out of every rare moment of sleep or calm not just to remember it but to actually feel it.

What was I going to do? What was I going to *do?* I felt suspended in a place only she had put me in and from which only I could get myself out.

"Mom," I heard Jack call. I snapped off the TV and went up to the boys' room, where the smell hit me instantly—nutty, salty, familiar—though he had been dry at night for well over a year.

"It's okay," I whispered, trying to get him out of the wet pajamas and sheets. He began shivering and I found him some clean pajamas. He was like a dead weight in my arms—still asleep, really—and I had a hard time handling him. I set him on the floor while I looked for clean sheets, and he curled into a little shivering ball, butt in the air. I didn't really know where to find new sheets, so I carried him down the stairs to my room.

"I love you, Daddy," he said, and kissed me passionately on the mouth. I pried his little arms from around my neck and lowered his body, dry and warm now, on what was, or used to be, Georgie's side of the bed.

After my separation from the Duke I remained with my profession as the only means of extricating myself from debt. How the debts piled up. I was at that time in so unsettled a state that I might fairly be called a citizen of the world, for all places appeared alike to me, provided they produced money.

I played well in the provinces—Exeter, Portsmouth, Southampton, Salisbury, Bath—but when I was back in London, preparing for Violante in Covent Garden, a very cruel article appeared in the Times. *I have saved it, Miss Williams, not for the harm it did but because I love candour and truth on all occasions and must not endeavour to leave anything out of my story. Thus, such an assault:*

"What share of public approbation should be permitted to one for whom it is impossible to feel any share of personal respect? Whose sons and daughters are now strangely allowed to move among the honourable people of England, received by the Sovereign, and starting in full appetite for Royal patronage, while their mother wanders, and is allowed to wander, from barn to barn, and from town to town, bringing shame on the art she practises, and double shame on those who must have it in their power to send her back to penitence and obscurity?"

Oh, Miss Williams, after such an attack by the Times *I despaired of appearing on the boards ever again. I have faced the hostility of the press and the public many times in my life, but it is one thing to face such hostility when one is young. I was fifty-one years old and by now very tired; I no longer had the strength to fight back.*

As I prepared to go on stage that evening, my legs were so unsteady I felt at times I would crumble. I feared addressing the audience, but I did not have to. I was bravoed several times before I even spoke, you see, and when one of the other actors' lines was, "You have an honest face and need not be ashamed of showing it anywhere," that blessed audience broke into a most fantastical applause.

I had the audience's support and protection. I had not offended them in any way by returning to my profession. Moreover, I had a most compleat triumph over the rascal in the Times; *his scurrility was of service to me as an actress. Now I found I could feel depressed in the green room, but the minute my foot touched the scenic boards I was rejuvenated. I began to feel that acting kept me alive. In fact, it kept me from thinking.*

*I*n the days Georgie was gone I trudged around the house, getting the boys dressed, making their oatmeal, finding their schoolbooks, relieved beyond words each morning when the key turned in the lock and Emma's hearty "Hello, young Martin boys" filled the house. Then I could escape to work, where the busy sameness of deadlines and meetings gave me a modicum of control, some feeling of moving forward in my life.

Nighttimes belonged to me alone, and they had a different tenor, not the impossible chaos of the daylight but the palpable emptiness of being without her.

I was with some seriousness trying on life without Georgie, and as happens when you are about to lose someone you love, my memory began to be assaulted by everything that was precious about her. Scenes from our life together played out in front of my eyes, years old, some of them. The day I moved in with her, for instance—carting my boxes of books and Hefty bags full of clothes up four flights of stairs to her top-floor brownstone apartment. How she loved that apartment, small but sunny with a wood-burning fireplace and a fire escape leading to the roof. Her father had found it for her when she first left home. My roommate was moving out, and I needed to either get a new roommate or find a smaller apartment, and Georgie said simply, *Live with me*. We had known each other days, only days. I was not an impulsive person, but Georgie made me impulsive.

We agreed we would just try it; she could kick me out at any time; we made jokes—toilet-seat infractions and snoring and all of that, keeping it light. The day I moved in we shared a bottle of wine on the fire escape, the smell of basil and rosemary and mint from her window box filling the air but not eclipsing her smell, Georgie's smell, the dizzying scent of this woman I so newly loved. We toasted each other, and she said, "I'm going to live here forever. With you."

I believed her.

I believed her.

⌒⅀⅂

Jack wet the bed again. It was the third time since Georgie had left, and though I had finally remembered to buy diapers I had forgotten to put one on him. His bed was drenched and I took him up to mine, dressing him in one of my T-shirts, rolling up the sleeves and letting the shirt trail to the floor like an evening gown. I put a diaper on him then. Half asleep, he fought me. "I am not a baby, I am not a baby," he cried, and though I'd bought a size called Super Jumbo, the diaper barely went around his waist. I felt as if I were diapering an adult.

I settled him into my bed, where he slept immediately, and lay down next to him. I was nearly back to sleep when another boy called out—my name this time, not hers.

I went back up to the boys' room.

"Dad," Fergus said, sitting up in bed, perfectly rational. "I'm a little bit sad. I miss Mom. I'm feeling a little nervous about when she's coming back."

If *she's coming back*, I thought. *What if she never does? What if I never let her?*

I sat next to Fergus on his bed and stroked his back as he tried to fall asleep. In the other bed, Liam stirred only briefly and then stayed very still.

These boys, these little barometers. Jack was wetting the bed, and Liam was hitting anything that moved, principally Jack, but Fergus was okay. For a five-year-old he was eerily articulate about his feelings and seemingly not distressed by the bad ones. Georgie said it was because he was exposed to grief so early, even before he was born. She was eight months pregnant with Fergus when her father died, his tiny human heart beating steadily inside her when the shock hit and the convulsive grief set in. She has always been convinced that what she was feeling gave Fergus his primal, and lasting, understanding of the world as a place where great loss was expected and miraculously survived.

Perhaps in a way he had been preparing for this his whole life. In that way he is like me. I think it must be unusual, but it seems to me I knew all along how it would feel to lose Georgie, the way you know even before you say your first "I love you" what song will be playing in your head when you break up.

Not long after Georgie and I had moved in together, one of my work colleagues had invited us out to his apartment in Jersey City for dinner. Stephen was my editor, quite senior to me at *Financial World* but around my age, and we had bonded through the discovery that we were both from central Illinois. His wife was an investment banker, a Harvard MBA, and together they were a formidable couple, a couple who had plans, plans that they weren't at all reluctant to discuss with us over dinner. Georgie and I, who at the time had no plans beyond where we would have brunch the next afternoon, if we had enough cash, listened politely and nodded, each with increasingly sinking, but opposite, feelings about our hosts. They referred to New York as a two-to-four-year stop, and then they would be *out*, because who wanted to spend longer than that in this dirty cesspool? They talked about the communities they wanted to *buy into*—Newton or Needham, outside Boston, or Lake Forest, outside Chicago, where she had grown up; they talked about starting a family; they talked about a ski condo in Sun Valley or a golf resort in Hilton Head.

As they talked, I grew anxious, almost despondent, thinking here was this guy, no older than I, who clearly knew what he wanted, and where and when, and with whom. He not only had plans, but investments to back them up, while all I had was an unpublished novel and a load of debt and a girl I loved who had roughly the same.

"Makes you kind of envious, doesn't it?" I asked Georgie later, when our hosts were doing the dishes and the two of us, drunk and inconsiderate, were slow-dancing to Elvis Costello in a living room that was bigger than our entire apartment.

"What makes you envious?" she asked in the combative tone I would now recognize instantly but was just learning to interpret then.

"Stephen and Maria," I said. "They've got it together."

"Plans schmans," Georgie said. "They might as well be planning their funerals."

I could have let it drop then, but maybe because I'd had too much to drink I persisted, and soon we were having a full-fledged argument, a quiet one laced with that special vehemence you reserve for fights about other people's lives.

"Come on," I said, "give them a break. They're nice people."

"Nice, yes. Who said they weren't *nice*?" Her voice indicated that being nice was possibly the worst crime you could ever be guilty of.

"What's wrong with being nice?" I asked.

"Nothing. They're nice, ordinary people."

"This may come as a big surprise to you, but most people in the world are ordinary." We had stopped dancing now and I stared at her. "And happy to be so," I added pointedly, thinking about my older brother, Dave, who had some mild disabilities—mild enough to feel constant frustration at his own limitations, severe enough so that no amount of love and care and therapy could help him fully overcome them. He and my parents would have loved for anyone to call him ordinary. And then there were my parents themselves, whom Georgie hadn't even met yet. They were the nicest, kindest people in the world, but kindness suddenly seemed a currency that held no value in Georgie's world. My dad with his State Farm job and yard work, my mom stitching pillows for the church bazaar—Georgie would see them only as ordinary, and I, by extension, was the same.

"I guess I'm just not as passionate about mediocrity as you are, Peter," Georgie said. It was the first cruel thing she had ever said to me.

"Maybe I'm not so terrified of being like everyone else," I said.

"I don't know how I can be with you if that's what you think," she said dramatically, and she turned and fled out the front door and down the stairs like a teenager. I made an excuse to Steve and Maria that she was sick and ran after her—it was late, we had been drinking, and this was unfamiliar territory. There was no way I was going to let her find her way home alone.

I followed from a distance as she walked Jersey City's ghostly streets, and just as she was about to take a wrong turn I caught up to her.

"This way," I said, and guided her to the train, where we had an interminable and silent wait in the station, sitting far apart, avoiding each other's eyes. On the train back to Manhattan and during the walk home, we didn't say a word. I was literally planning how I would pack up my stuff the next day and where I might go.

But in the morning I woke to Georgie leaning over me. "I'm so sorry," she said. "Sorry sorry sorry," and she had tears in her eyes. "You're the mild-mannered reporter for the *Daily Planet* and I'm the bitch queen from hell. Oh, Peter, forgive me."

The abject apology, the makeup sex, the makeup brunch after the makeup sex, the immediate easing of tension into equilibrium. It was the first time I needed to forgive her, and of course I did. There was never any doubt.

But this time, when it should have been harder to walk away because of all we had gathered in those years together, I had no idea how I would be able to stay.

It reached my ears at this time that the queen was afraid I should publish the Duke's letters to my own purposes, and I was so shocked by this accusation that I immediately sent the letters, all of them, to the royal advisors and asked them to no more entertain the idea that I should make improper use of them. There were hundreds of letters, Miss Williams, as you can imagine, nearly twenty years of correspondence, and when the Duke and I were apart we wrote to each other almost daily. Who knows what has become of those letters now. I believe they were burned, all of them. My greatest loss now is that I have nothing left of the Duke's private words to me.

Letters were now the only way I could reach my children, and I wrote every day to each of them, wishing it were as easy to pack myself up in a packet to have one look at my dear ones. Yet from Bushy I scarcely ever heard, and when I did it appeared quite an effort for the children and the few lines so unsatisfactory that they brought more disappointment and mortification with them than anything else. I did not deserve this neglect, but whether present or absent my children must ever be equally dear to me.

The younger boys were all at school now, and as soon as they reached the age of eleven, they would be sent, like their elder brothers, to the army or navy. Henry was already in the Baltic, serving under the Duke's friend Admiral Keats, and I had not seen him for two years as such. It was too long to lose the society of a dear child like Henry, but we must give up our children to the world.

George, in Portugal, had a horse shot under him and was running in the road until Colonel Hawker found him another. Lovely George, his reputation should be a fine soft pillow for his head for many years to come.

The Duke had always said to me, "We have five boys, my dear, and must look forward to a life of constant anxiety and suspense!"

I worked two more seasons in the provinces, with a winter at Covent Garden in between, and then I retired. I began to visit the younger boys at school, I attended my older daughters' bedsides when they gave birth, and I became a proper soldiers' mother, making it my principal aim to spend time with George and Henry before they were to sail for India.

It was the end of August, in my fifty-fourth year, when I left the stage for good.

That, of course, was less than a year ago, Miss Williams, and if you have the time I will tell you what has befallen me since then.

*M*rs. Jordan.

  She had changed Georgie's life, and now she seemed the only real person left in it.

 In her hotel room, Georgie couldn't sleep; felt utterly alone; waited for the appointed hour each day when the boys would be home from school and she could talk to them. On the stage, even in the dressing room before and after the show, she felt secure, accompanied, not guilty of all she knew she was guilty of. She started getting to the theater earlier each night, and staying in her dressing room afterward until the stage manager insisted it was time to lock up and drive her home.

 She had not seen Piers in a week. A week's time was all that had passed since he drove her home from Dorset. She had told him she didn't want to see him, and yet she had found herself disappointed that he was honoring her wishes. That he could so easily take no for an answer was, she supposed, a little insulting. It was what she wanted, and yet—

 And yet—

On Saturday evening, a couple of hours before the show, Piers appeared at her dressing room door.

She stared at him in his wrinkled khakis and faded blue T-shirt that looked as if it had seen a thousand washes. He looked good. She felt a shyness, a shyness tight with desire.

"I didn't know you were coming," she said.

"May I come in?"

She hesitated, then nodded and stood aside to let him enter.

Her dressing room in the tithe barn was large and inviting, almost a lounge, with faded green sofas and yards of gold brocade fabric draped from the walls in imitation of curtains, though there were of course no windows.

Piers sat down on one of the sofas. She took a seat across from him. "I went to the hotel first," he said.

"No," she said. "I prefer to be here."

He nodded and said, "I need to talk to you about the play."

"The play?" She felt stiff, as if they were conducting some sort of formal interview.

"I've decided to make one or two changes," he said.

"And what would those be?"

He waited a beat, then smiled gently. "I've rewritten the ending."

"Oh?"

"I came round. Call me a thick-headed bastard, but you've shown it to me, Georgie. You were absolutely right all along."

Aha, she might have said if things had gone differently, *I told you so,* or *Glad you've finally seen the light,* teasing, flirtatious comments that fit the relationship they once had. But that wasn't the way they talked to each other any longer.

He placed an envelope in front of her. "It might not be exactly as you would have done, but I think you'll be quite happy."

"Why now?" she asked. "There are so few performances left."

"I don't expect you to take it on board right away. We can finish up the run as it is if you like. But when you have a moment take a look and see what you think."

Georgie's eyes widened. She waited.

"Nicola's friend Richard has come through for us and agreed to produce a limited West End run in September."

"That's fantastic," Georgie said.

"It is," he said. "It is."

He was quiet for a moment, fiddling with the coat on his lap. He was withholding something, she could tell. Even in a personality that seemed all about withholding, she could tell there was something more he had to tell her. He reached out as if to take her hand, and she drew back. She had not imagined how easy it might be to fall back into him, to make his gesture lead forward to a place they had so recently been and where he appeared willing to return. But she wouldn't do it. No matter what, she would not. It was an act of will, she had decided. She would not respond to his touch.

"But?" she said.

"It's a tricky show to produce. Despite the excellent notices you've gotten, the very respectable houses, a one-woman show in the West End is an enormous risk."

"Oh," Georgie said. She knew what was coming, but waited to hear him tell it anyway.

Piers seemed uncharacteristically flustered. "Richard feels to stand a chance we need a huge name, someone audiences will flock to see," he said, pausing and wincing slightly. "I'm sorry to have to tell you this, Georgie. You've been phenomenal. You originated the part, you made Mrs. Jordan live. I see now how comparatively easy my job was. All I had to do was piece together the story of her life. You had to convince people they knew what it was like to be in the same room with her."

"And yet you're firing me anyway?" Georgie asked.

He looked uncomfortable. "It's out of my hands, obviously. To make the kind of money he's got to make—to get enough bums on enough seats—he's got to give them a grande dame of the British theater. He's going after Helen Mirren, if she's available. Judi Dench if not Helen Mirren." He smiled tenderly. "You were always too young for the part, anyway."

"Right," Georgie said curtly.

They wanted to offer her the understudy, Piers said, a good wage, a steady run, and possibly they could cut a deal to guarantee her the Wednesday matinees.

"You can think about it," he said. "I know it's a lot to take in right now."

When she didn't reply, he said, "Maybe I should have waited until after the show. I am not known for my impeccable timing, as you know."

"It doesn't matter," Georgie said. She found herself laughing. With all she had risked, maybe even lost, she was now losing Mrs. Jordan, too.

"What is it?" Piers asked. "What's so funny?"

"Nothing," she said. "A bad dream. A really awful practical joke. I guess a nightmare."

The quizzical look stayed on his face for a moment. "Look, Georgie," he said. "I'm sure you're thinking—to be honest, I have no idea what you're thinking—but I'm sorry about"—he waved his hands vaguely—"all this. It's hell, I know, and if I could help you put it right I would."

"It's not your problem," she said dismissively. They stared at each other for a few moments, saying nothing. Georgie was thinking that she had never before understood people who were able to divorce and remarry quickly, saying goodbye to one part of their lives and moving, hopefully, cheerfully, onto another. She had never understood how the Duke could close the door on twenty years with Mrs. Jordan—and ten children!—and start his life anew without ever seeing Mrs. Jordan again. Now, for the first time, she could almost grasp it. She could imagine cutting me out of her life and turning toward him, because what she had with me seemed beyond repair while with him there was an unblemished record, a land of infinite possibilities.

And yet as soon as she was able to imagine it, she knew that wasn't what she wanted. She didn't want to go with him. She wanted me, she still did; she wanted her old life back, and she would fight for it.

As Piers left her dressing room to become part of the audience for the evening's show, she did not rise from her sofa but instead watched him go as if he were the one onstage, making his exit, and she in the third row. She was thinking, *I could do this, this is another life I could live, or at least try out,* but she quelled her impulse to touch him or say anything else, and instead let desire for him pass through her body and slip cleanly and permanently away.

I was but barely retired when a horrible circumstance burst upon me like a thunderstorm. My name, which has always been a passport everywhere, was now being used by my daughter Dodee's husband to empty my bank account and enter into huge debts. Having no way of paying these very pressing demands, I faced immediate arrest, and in order to save Dodee's family from utter ruin I was advised to go abroad. I sold my furniture in the first instance and quit London for France.

I expected to stop in France for ten days but it has now been nearly a year, Miss Williams, and I am still unable to return to England for fear of being arrested. The solicitors tell me I need a list of creditors in order to begin paying off the debts, but I can find no one in England who will help me with such a list. All my life I have been too trusting, Miss Williams, and now for that easy quality I must pay this shocking price.

I find France an odious place and this house large, gloomy, and cold, almost in a state of dilapidation. No English comforts solace me here; instead the house echoes the gloomy habit of my soul.

My weak hand is scarcely able to trace the still more feeble efforts of my mind. I write to everybody from this place—but no answer.

Admirers occasionally discover who I am and come by, as you have,

Miss Williams, but mostly I am alone with Miss Sketchley, my main oc-
cupation being to write each and every day to my children and to wait and
to hope for letters to arrive from them.

And so my story has journeyed to the present moment, and it only re-
mains to be seen what will happen next. I only wish this unfortunate affair
would finish. I am not well, Miss Williams. I have pains and shortness of
breath. I have become weak, very weak.

Even now I feel a regard for the Duke I cannot conquer, and as I wait
here in my exile I believe that surely I may expect some return of gratitude
from a man who by a single act could relieve these fears that are nearly
unsupportable.

A fter the show, Georgie returned to her dressing room and opened the envelope Piers had left for her. What he had given her was not just the new ending but an entire playscript, printed on heavy cream-colored paper and nicely bound.

He had signed the title page:

For Georgie—Mrs Jordan, Shakespeare's Woman, Muse,
Even before I knew you,
I wrote this for you.
For you. For you. For you.

All my love,
Piers

There was a knock on the door. She expected it to be Piers again, but it was Chris, the stage manager.

"Did you know when you wanted to go back?" he asked.

"Not soon," she said vaguely, eyes on the script.

"It's just that I have one or two minor repairs to do to the set, and I can either run you back to the hotel now or you can wait—"

"I'll wait," Georgie said. "I'm in no hurry. Just let me know when you're done."

She boiled some water in the electric kettle and made herself a cup of tea, then sat down to read the play again. She didn't rush to the new ending but began at the beginning and read the whole play, start to finish, just as she had the very first time in our little sitting room. It didn't matter that she had just finished performing the play or that, until the final pages, she knew every word by heart. She was happy to read Mrs. Jordan's story again, and an hour and a half later, when she stopped reading, her face was wet with tears.

How she loved this play, this character, this woman whose story no longer ended in loneliness and despair in a foreign country but instead on the stage, where she was adored. Maybe it was Piers's apology, she thought, this new ending her consolation for losing both of her roles at once. Yet she knew that he would not have made the change if he did not believe it was the ending his play deserved.

Piers had written a new ending for Georgie, and now she hoped that I would do the same. She was holding vigil at the deathbed of our marriage, praying that our story would not end where it now seemed destined to end.

In truth, our ending had not yet been written. It was still to come, and if I could go back in time, I would gladly give Piers my wife, let him have her and have her and have her, let the story end there instead of carrying on to an ending none of us would ever have written or be able to bear.

Georgie returned to London the next day. Our arrangement was that she would stay at Graham's, but pick up the boys from school each day and spend time with them at our house until just before I was due home. It was a solution. Of course I could not keep the boys from their mother. I can't honestly remember now what we told them—something about late performances, early-morning rehearsals, Georgie needing to stay somewhere else. Who knows what lies we gave them? They were smart boys. They knew something was deeply wrong.

Before she left for Dorset at the end of the week, Georgie insisted on talking to me in person, and I agreed. I felt an absurd nervousness about seeing her. I paced the blocks around the restaurant where we were to meet, working against my nature to try to be late, staying away until I was sure she would be there. I wanted somehow to see her first, to watch her through the restaurant window as I approached and study her before she noticed me.

The third time I passed she was there, seated at a table in the window. Carefully dressed, looking beautiful and a little tired, she sat up straight, scrutinizing the menu as if it held the measure of some secret she longed to know. I felt a little sob rise in my throat as I looked at her, and almost as if she heard that odd strangled noise through the pane of glass, she looked up. She beamed at me, and I realized that was exactly what I was hoping for—her face made lustrous by the small event of her eyes landing on me. Momentarily, everything fell away, and I was convinced that to make that look appear on her face again, and again, was possibly my best reason for being alive.

I walked in, pushing past the hostess, who wanted to take my coat, going directly to Georgie. She was standing by this point, and smiling; she reached her arms out to me. When I didn't stiffen or pull back as I usually did, she nestled into me and held on.

All I wanted to do was to keep holding her, not stop, never have to begin a conversation that could only end with bitterness, anger, regret.

When I did begin to speak, I chose safely. I chose the children.

"How has it been," I asked. "Seeing them?"

"Great!" she said. "God, I missed them so much. I felt like I'd been away a year."

"Did Liam tell you he made a goal?"

"He did?" she asked. "He didn't tell me that." She had that expression on her face, the familiar one where she looked as if she had just awakened and was about to start puzzling through some complicated nuclear physics problem. A huge smile burst out of the confusion. "He did?"

"Yes, his first one, EVER. You have to say it like that—EVER. He was so proud."

"So am I," she said. "I guess the magic throw-up-inducing wizard Thibaud has lost some of his magical powers?"

"Actually, he hasn't," I said. "However, in an extraordinary stroke of luck, Liam's own powers have appeared to become 'more magicaler.' That's the explanation I got, anyway."

"Oh," she said. "Why didn't he tell me? They never tell me anything. You should hear those phone calls while I'm away! They just keep passing the phone back and forth, and no one ever says anything much. Fergus keeps asking, 'When are you coming home?' in this complete monotone as if he couldn't care less. And Jack laughs or makes fart noises and says, 'What? What? What? What?' over and over again and never listens to the answers anyway. I end up talking to Emma more than anyone else, and she's almost as bad as they are." Here Georgie put on Emma's Yorkshire accent. "'Now let me just pop this into the oven and then I'm on to helping Fergus with his maths, aren't I, Fergus?'" Her monologue over, Georgie looked to me, smiling, expecting a reaction. I felt suddenly cold, as if her familiarity was uncalled for.

We fell quiet until the waitress appeared and we ordered starters and a bottle of wine. I changed the subject.

"How's the show?" I asked.

"Oh," she said. At first I thought she was reluctant to talk about it at all because she wanted to prove that her family was at the center of her life now, her work merely peripheral. When she asked, "Bad news or good?" I realized she had something else to tell me.

"Whichever you prefer," I said.

"Okay," she said. "I'll present it the way it was presented to me. They've changed the ending to the play."

They—Piers.

"Oh, have they?" I asked.

"Yes. It's more uplifting now, truer to Mrs. Jordan as an artist. You know I've been fighting for this all along."

"Good," I managed, while wanting to rage against her. That she could talk about work, that she was really talking about *him*. I had asked and she was answering, but I was just beginning to learn what such a conversation could take out of me.

"The further good news is that they've got somebody who wants to produce the show on the West End," Georgie said.

"Great," I said neutrally, mouth dry as sand. *Fuck it,* I could have said, and been the guy who got up from the table and walked away. Instead I picked up my glass and drank some of my wine.

"But that's closely connected to the bad news." She pursed her lips. "I'm not keeping the part. They can't fill a house that big for a one-woman show unless it's somebody massively famous." She looked down, staring at the bread on her plate, then up at me tentatively. "And in case you hadn't noticed, I'm not massively famous."

"I'm sorry," I said.

"Thank you," she said, deliberately showing me that she would not take anything I said for granted. "They've offered me understudy," she said slowly.

"Oh," I said, then paused and asked, "What are you going to do?"

"About what?" she asked, as if jostled from another conversation.

"The understudy thing."

"I don't know," she said. "Mrs. Jordan. I'd like to stay with her, the money's not bad, but—" Her eyes took on a demure cast that had nothing to do with who she really was. "A lot depends on you," she said.

"Oh, come on," I said. "Don't think that putting me in charge of your career is going to make it all better." These were the first bitter words I had spoken all evening, and with them came a reluctant weariness that spun around on itself and tripled, quadrupled the hostility that was already there at the table.

I could tell she wanted to change the subject, but it was like wartime—there was no other subject. After a moment she said, "What I mean is, I would give up everything if you'd forgive me."

"Really?" I said. "Everything? That's a dangerous pronouncement."

"I mean it," she said.

"No you don't," I said. "If I were such a valuable commodity, you would have made sure you kept me in the first place."

She reached across the table and took my hand. "You're what I want," she said. "You and the boys. I don't want to lose you, Peter, for heaven's sake. Look at everything we have together."

"So I'm part of a package?" I asked. "'Everything.' The adoring husband and the cherubic little boys, waiting in the wings."

"Peter, please."

"I don't believe you, Georgie. I can't believe you. Why would you give it all up? It's the only place you're happy. I've seen it with my own eyes."

I waited for her contradiction. Hoped for it.

While I waited for her to speak, I did nothing but study her face.

And then, in the way a story that had been for such a long time about one thing can suddenly become about something else, she said, "The truth is, Peter, I may never have a part this good again, but I've got to spend the rest of my life trying."

Instead of disappointment, her words brought a beautiful relief. For once at least I knew she was telling the truth. It was out in the open. She could have resorted to heroic measures if she thought by doing so she could keep me. But even Mrs. Jordan had shown her that giving up the work you love for the man you love is no answer. Maybe the truth was that I was happiest when we were in New Jersey because there were no directors or playwrights or other actors to compete with for her, no audience but me. And she was happiest . . .

We both knew exactly where she was happiest.

"It was so much easier when we both just had our work," she said. "In New York. Your writing. My acting. Just waking up every day with that on our minds."

"That and how broke we were."

"And that horrific mouse problem."

"And more than a few roaches."

I smiled back at her, willing at that moment to sacrifice decades of my life to be back within the exposed brick walls of that tiny walk-up apartment. To start things over. I wondered how it was that so many seemingly reasonable decisions made over the years had led us so far from there.

"I can do both, Peter," Georgie said. "I know I can. That was something separate, that thing with Piers. I lost my mind. I have no excuses. But it's over, I promise you that, and if you give me a chance I'll make it up to you." She had taken my hand and was leaning over the table toward me. I wanted her so much just then.

"I can't sleep," she said. "I can't eat. I can't survive without the boys. I need our family. I just need you to take me back." Her eyes searched mine. "It's me, Peter," she said. "Here I am. Nothing's changed."

"Everything's changed." I spoke as if through anesthesia, a thick low cloud that both impeded my ability to think and kept me alive.

We ordered another bottle of wine, and I found myself trying to regain my resolve, my cold distance, empty my heart. But I couldn't. It was too full of Georgie, she was everywhere in it, all those years together, all the moments that she and I alone had ever known. I began to think the only way to bear it was to try to be those people again.

After dinner, she said to me, simply, "Please," looking stricken, looking as if she were clinging to the edge of the world, and because I had loved her so much and because I did still, I found a taxi and I took her home with me, and to bed with me, where we made love for the first time since—

Since.

I fought him as I made love to her, fought his presence, his imprint on her body, the times he had touched her, the kisses he had left on her skin. I fought to feel the same about her, crying and baring my teeth against her neck until finally my excitement, my cheap relief, took over and I was able to stay there with her, in our bed, her body my tenderest home.

*I*n the morning I awoke first and watched her sleeping. In every room we have ever shared she has slept on the same side of the bed. And there she was, as always, next to me, except that now he was there between us.

"Good morning," I said softly, but she didn't stir until a few minutes later, when Liam barreled into the room, followed by Jack, who was shrieking, "He took my diaper. He took my broken diaper."

"Ha ha," Liam said, throwing the squidgy diaper into the air.

"Boys," I said. "Stop it."

"Mommy's here," Jack said, forgetting about the diaper. "Mommy, you here?"

"Yes, darling," Georgie said, holding out her arms. "I'm here."

"Hooray!" Jack said, and Liam joined in, and soon Fergus was there, too, and they were all in our bed, laughing and tickling us, and everyone seemed to forget that the boys needed to get to school, and I to work, and Georgie—back to Dorset.

"It's like Christmas morning," Georgie said to me. "Let's make it Christmas morning, Peter. Can you go in a little late? Can I take you all out to breakfast? It's not going to kill them to miss the first hour or so of school."

"Breakfast!" Liam yelled. "I like breakfast!"

We went to a little place off Kensington High Street where we sat in the sunny back room and had toast and tea and juice. Then we walked the boys to school through the park, allowing them to stop and climb their favorite tree. It was a glorious morning in London, sunny, fresh, everything in full bloom, but with enough memory of the wet winter still around to inspire disproportionate gratitude. I felt an unaccountable sense of well-being, perhaps just the happiness of wanting to be happy.

I couldn't help but see us as anyone passing by might have seen us that morning: a beautiful woman holding hands with her nice-looking husband, three smiling boys in gray shorts and red sweaters jostling and racing and calling to each other as they made their way across Kensington Gardens. There must have been hundreds of families walking around London that same day presenting to the world a picture of happiness many degrees variant from the reality they held in their hearts.

I would like to end with that happy family, one night's reunion offering them hope that they would stay together. They might have made it; they had a chance; I have seen couples pull back from the brink for less.

I wish I could end there, in Kensington Gardens, the boys shaking the newly leafed branches of that favorite tree, Georgie calling, "Be careful!" and me looking at my watch, needing to go to work but not wanting to tear myself away.

All the normal things of normal life appeared to be back, but underneath there was also this wondering if what seemed like a reconciliation could possibly be one. Because even if you return to each other, bodies fitting together again, lives tessellated in all the old places, there's still this terrible pulling at any bit of happiness you can muster. It wasn't only that what happened might happen again; it was also still the fact that it had happened at all.

Even though I was with her, even though she walked through the park next to me and held my hand, there was a watchfulness, the furtive mistrust you would show a former addict or a teenaged son who had been in trouble. A watchfulness that between lovers can only, eventually, enrage.

I arrived home late that night after a business dinner. Georgie had returned to Dorset, the boys were in bed, and Emma was in the sitting room with her coat on her lap, wearing extra makeup and dressed to go dancing. She jumped to her feet as soon as I came in. I must have been later than she had expected, but I felt too drained to start up a conversation or even apologize. It occurred to me suddenly, fleetingly, that Emma might not be very happy with her job. Maybe the hours were too long now, or the demands too great, or the boys' recent behavior more than she could take. What would I do if she quit? I was completely dependent on her. I needed to think about making sure she was happy, but it was the last thing I had patience for just then. I thanked her excessively as she hurried off, and I had some vague thought in my head about giving her a raise. God, she was so young! In the mess Georgie had created, my family was now being held together by a twenty-year-old.

I went upstairs to take off my suit and then sat on the bed to let utter exhaustion wash over me. The day had felt so long, so multifaceted, as if lived by six different men. Which man was I? The one who seemed to have welcomed his wife back into his family that morning, or the one who now, when spying the watch Georgie had left on the bedside table, wanted nothing more than to hurl it against the wall and shatter the crystal?

I realized this was my story now—no longer Georgie's—because it had become about what I was going to do, how I was going to behave, whether I would truly forgive her or find a way to make her pay. More than anything, I didn't want it to be my story. I found it much easier to tell hers.

I fell asleep quickly but was awakened in the deep night by Liam standing at my bedside.

"Mom? Mom?" he said.

"It's okay, Liam," I said.

"Where's my mom?" he asked. "Where's my mommy?"

"Ssssh," I said, holding him, but he pulled away.

"I miss my mommy," he said, as if I were some casual babysitter, practically a stranger.

"She'll be back soon," I said.

I brought him into bed with me, hoping he would go back to sleep, but both of us were still awake when Jack appeared, shivering and wet, a little while later. Emma had forgotten to put a diaper on him, or maybe he had fought her too much and she had given up.

"God damn it," I said, "not again." I pushed him away to prevent him from climbing into bed with his pee-soaked pajamas, and perhaps I handled him more roughly than I should have. He suddenly began to scream as if I were killing him.

"Mommy," he cried. "I want my mommy."

"Oh, Jacky," I said, bending down to hug him. He pulled away and cried harder, and Liam began to cry as well.

"This is crazy, guys," I said. "Do you miss your mom so much?"

"Yes, yes, yes!" they cried, and hugged me.

"Okay, my boys," I said, before I was awake enough to assess what I was saying, "we'll go and see her."

"Yes!" Jack yelled.

"Now back to bed," I said.

"But you said we could go see Mommy," he said.

"Yes," I said. "But not right now. It's nighttime."

"But you said," Jack said, and his lips started quivering.

"Don't cry," I said. "Please don't cry." The desperation in my voice served to hasten the tears, and I held him wearily, rocking him back and forth, feeling as if I had spent, and would continue to spend, every night of my life calming one or another of my sons.

I could feel the wetness from his pajamas soaking into mine. "We have to change your clothes," I chanted. "We have to change your clothes." He held on tightly as I tried to pry his hands from my neck, and I pulled at him with increasing force until he finally went limp and tumbled onto the floor.

He began sobbing piteously again. I had made things worse instead of better, and he turned away from me. Liam made some attempt to comfort his brother, and I went into the bathroom to try to get hold of myself. I threw cold water on my face and rubbed my tense, pale jaw. Just as I felt myself calming slightly, I could hear Liam's soothing voice turn combative, and I walked back into the bedroom to find the boys in a knot on the floor.

"Stop it," I said, and then, louder, "Stop it now."

The boys barely glanced at me. Outside I could hear several young voices in the street, a group of girls laughing and talking loudly as they came home late from the clubs.

"Stop it!" I said again. The anger rose mercurially inside me, and without a thought I picked up Georgie's watch and hurled it as hard as I could at the open bedroom window. The watch didn't go out the window but instead hit the glass above it with a crack that was loud enough to make the boys stop fighting.

"What happened?" Liam asked. "What was that big big crash?"

My heart beat madly. I couldn't believe how angry I had become, or how quickly. I felt childish, but better, and I was reminded of someone I knew in college who had once keyed obscenities all over the car of the girlfriend who cheated on him. *It felt great,* he told me afterward, *it just felt so great.*

"What happened, Daddy?" Jack asked.

"Nothing," I answered. "Nothing at all."

The next day I took all three boys down to Dorset on the train. It was a grand adventure for them—swapping seats every three minutes, using the "lavatory" (as they had been taught to call it in school), walking through the speeding, lurching carriages to the dining car. Their collective nighttime terror had been replaced by high jinks and fun, and I found myself almost annoyed that they no longer seemed so desperate and that I had reacted so fiercely to their behavior. I was beginning to mistrust my instincts as a father, which now seemed almost as volatile as my feelings toward my wife.

Once again I set out to surprise Georgie, but this time it was different. Just as we reached the hotel after the short walk from the train station, we saw her approaching from the other direction, her arms full of packages. She saw us first and called our names, and the boys, who only seconds before had been complaining about the long walk, started running down the narrow sidewalk toward her.

"Be careful," I shouted. There wasn't much room on the sidewalk, and the cars on the road were so close.

"Mommy," the boys all yelled, competing to see who could get to her first. They seemed to wrap themselves around her, and she hugged all of them, laughing at the crushed packages. I thought, *No, she is not a complete ogre, she is a woman who does love her family.*

"I'm so glad you came," she was telling them. "I missed you all so much."

"Can we come see your movie?" Jack asked.

"It's not a movie," she said. "It's a play, remember?"

"And it's not for children," I said. "We'll do something fun while Mommy's in the play, and then we can see her when it's over."

"It would be great if you could come, Peter," Georgie said. "I'm trying out the new ending for the first time tonight."

I swallowed the bitterness that was ready at my lips. "What am I going to do with them?" I asked.

"Maybe we can get a babysitter. Someone to watch them in my room in the hotel, don't you think?"

"That would be kind of weird," I said.

"I could ask at the hotel desk——"

"No," I said dismissively. "I don't need to see the play again. I'll stay with them."

"Okay, then," Georgie said. She was looking at me carefully, trying to read my expression.

"Let's get away from the road," I said. "It's dangerous."

"I have the perfect place," Georgie said. "It's where I usually go right about now to get dinner before the show." She turned her attention toward the boys again. "Do you want to come have some fish-and-chips with me?"

"Yes," they all cried, though they had eaten nonstop on the train, and she led us all away from the center of town on a ten-minute walk to a pub, the Royal Oak.

"What I love about this place is that it seems like the edge of civilization," Georgie said when we got there. She pointed me back toward town, the crowded assemblage of brown brick buildings and cobblestone streets, then turned me in the other direction so that all I could see was green countryside, the tithe barn the only building visible in the distance. "See?"

The boys began to shriek when they saw that the pub had a playground in the back garden and though it was windy, and getting colder, we sat outside so that they could play.

"What a great combination," I said, drinking a pint of lager and watching the boys climb up a ladder, slide down a slide, and then pile, all three, precipitously on a rusty metal duck.

"They probably get more business this way," Georgie said. "People don't need to pay for a babysitter, they just bring the kids along."

"Some things the English do really well," I said. "Can you imagine this idea flying in the puritanical U.S.A.? 'Let your children play on our rusty play equipment while you get blotto!'"

We could not get the boys to eat anything, or even to sit down with us. Occasionally Liam ran by, yelling, "We are having FUN!"

"This cold air is not the greatest thing for my voice," Georgie said, but did not suggest moving inside. We sat side by side at a picnic table so we could both keep our eyes on the boys. Our conversation remained light, not at all strained, and only when she said again, "I wish you could be in the audience tonight, Peter," did I feel my body clench with anger.

A few more cars entered the parking lot. The pub began to fill up. A barmaid brought us some cutlery and a bottle of ketchup, and later our dinner, but otherwise we remained alone outside, and undisturbed. The sky turned to pinks and oranges; the boys appeared as silhouettes, three dark figures in perpetual motion against the sunset. I began to have the feeling that there was nothing in the world besides my family, that my family was the world, or all the world I needed, so complete, so contained, so mine.

It was not the first time in my life I had had that feeling, but I distinctly remember having it then because it was going to be the last.

After Georgie and I finished dinner, the boys and I walked the further half-mile to the theater with her.

"This is a *church*," Liam said when we walked into the tithe barn.

"It's not a church," Georgie said. "Could you do this in a church?" She took off running and whooping and the boys ran after her, laughing and trying to imitate her.

She let them run around the stage for a few minutes, ignoring the anxious looks of the stage manager, and then she took us into her dressing room.

"Who . . . who lives here, whose, whose . . . house is this?" Fergus asked, confused by the elegant look of the room.

"It's no one's house," Georgie said. She launched into a singsongy kind of story. "A long time ago there was a very famous actress who was supposed to act in a play here but she thought she was too important to act in a *barn*. She finally said she would only do it on one condition: her dressing room had to look *exactly* like her living room at home. So they put in all these fancy drapes and couches and that cozy little fireplace, and all those paintings, and it's stayed this way ever since."

"Famous actresses can be very demanding," I said.

The boys busied themselves jumping from couch to couch, and Georgie didn't stop them. Perhaps because she was nearing the end of the run she was feeling confident and relaxed. I had never seen her so calm before a performance.

The boys weren't very interested in seeing Georgie put on her makeup, but they did manage to sit still and watch. Just after she finished, there was a knock on the door.

Nicola poked her head in. "Oh, sorry," she said. "I didn't know..." Her voice trailed off.

That the cuckold husband was here? I thought. I suddenly appreciated Nicola's British sensibility. An American director might have given me deep, soulful looks full of pity and understanding, but Nicola had a *Tough break, old chap; let's get on with it* air about her that was actually more comforting.

"Tom wants to have a word with you about the lighting," she told Georgie. "He's had an idea about the spots for the new ending. And the house is opening momentarily."

"I'll be there in a sec," Georgie said. "Let me just say goodbye to my family."

"Right," Nicola said.

"Did you see that?" Georgie asked after Nicola had gone. "She didn't even acknowledge the children. She didn't even look at them. So typical."

"Come on, boys," I said. "Say goodbye to Mommy. We have to go now."

"Bye, Mommy," Fergus said. "Break your leg."

"I will, darling."

"I have to go pee," Jack said.

"Me, too," Liam said.

"You can wait until we get back to the pub," I said.

"No, I can't," Jack wailed. "I have to go poo."

"It's okay," Georgie said. "You can use the bathroom here and then sneak out the back. I'll show you the secret way out."

Fergus and I followed her while the twins fought over the toilet. She showed us a small wooden staircase in the area outside her dressing room. "If you go up that staircase and then down the other one, you'll go straight outside without traipsing through the theater. It's an old dovecote or something." She bent down and gave Fergus another hug. "I love you, baby," she said.

"I love you too, Mommy," he said.

I love you, she mouthed to me over his head, and then she was gone.

Back in the dressing room we could hear Jack singing "Old Mac-Donald Had a Farm," which meant he was probably still sitting on the toilet. Liam was quiet; I suspected he was making faces at himself in the mirror.

Fergus busied himself jumping from couch to couch again, and I wandered idly around Georgie's dressing room. On her dressing table was a picture of the boys, and tucked into the mirror was the playbill from her first paying role—an off-off-Broadway revival of *Sweeney Todd*. It was her good-luck charm. The script of *Shakespeare's Woman* was there, too, and I picked it up. It was the new copy, and I saw the handwritten note on the front. Piers's dedication to Georgie.

I could feel the physical changes as I read Piers's words, the wild acceleration of my heart, the drumming around my ears as the adrenaline and cortisol rose at rapid pace through my body.

"Daddy," Fergus said. "What's the matter? Daddy?"

The rage descended on me, took me over as I held the manuscript with hands that were shaking and read again the words that would destroy us.

For Georgie—Mrs Jordan, Shakespeare's Woman, Muse,
Even before I knew you,
I wrote this for you.
For you. For you. For you.

All my love,
Piers

Mrs Jordan: the whole of my name is a lie, a stage name if you prefer that gentler thought.

Georgie began her performance that night just as she had every night. It was a smaller house than usual—a cold night, late in the run—but full of attentive people. She felt them with her immediately, and they followed Mrs. Jordan all the way to the end—the ending he had changed for her—when she lay on a faded gold silk divan, surrounded by papers, letters, writing tablets, books.

I grow weaker so that I can scarcely rise from this sofa.

Yes, the doctor has been here. He says it is the jaundice, la maladie noire.

Past twelve and still no letters?

She called offstage:

Miss Sketchley, would you please go into the village and look again?

She turned back to her audience—the adoring visitor who had sought out the famous actress as she spent her last days in France:

It is not, believe me, the feelings of pride, avarice, or the absence of those comforts I have all my life been accustomed to, that is killing me by inches; it is the loss of my only remaining comfort, the hope I used to live on from time to time, of seeing my children.

Ten thousand thousand thanks, my dear friend, for this charitable visit. You revive my spirits and for a period waft me back to my own dear native country, my beloved theatrical past. Viola. The Country Girl. Dear Rosalind.

And here, where she might have died in the play's earlier version, she used her arms to pull herself up. The dying woman, the woman who had lost everything—children, lover, money, home—found some performance left in her, drew some strength from Rosalind, her most treasured role.

The poor world is almost six thousand years old, and in all this time there was not any man died in his own person, videlicet, in a love-cause. Troilus had his brains dashed out with a Grecian club, yet he did what he could to die before, and he is one of the patterns of love. Leander, he would have lived many a fair year though Hero had turned nun, if it had not been for a hot midsummer night, for, good youth, he went but forth to wash him in the Hellespont and, being taken with the cramp, was drowned, and the foolish chroniclers of that age found it was Hero of Sestos. But these are all lies. Men have died from time to time, and worms have eaten them, but not for love.

She let a playful grin show through Mrs. Jordan's age and pain, the regal bearing of her body still there despite the sickness. She smiled, head back, eyes closed; she smiled as if she knew everything in the world there was to know. And then came her finish.

The applause. Miss Williams, do you hear it? There it is, do you hear it? Oh, internal exultation. It has always been a delight for me, a delight that borders on ecstasy.

Her face clouded over and her posture slackened as she turned toward her visitor one last time. After a pause, she spoke her final lines.

No. No. I shall never hear it again.

She lowered her face, but then of course she did hear the applause because as the curtain fell and then rose again, everyone in the theater stood and cheered and clapped for Georgie.

She was finished; it was her last performance; she left Mrs. Jordan and smiled at them all.

The pub was packed and noisy by the time the boys and I returned to it. It had taken us almost a half-hour just to walk from the tithe barn. The boys, now hungry, were also tired and cold, their sluggishness at odds with my racing mind and heart. I barked orders at them, trying to keep them moving. They complained endlessly; I alternated carrying Jack and Liam on my shoulders; Fergus started to cry. At one point I really didn't know how I was going to get the three of them across the field to the pub.

When we finally got there, I stood in line at the bar to order them dinner while they busied themselves at the jukebox, pushing buttons and pretending to choose songs, though none of them knew how to read.

I found a table in the family dining room, and the boys joined me once their food arrived. They were so hungry that they actually ate, didn't fight, barely even talked, and I was able to sit and drink my pint in something resembling peace.

The glass in my hand began to shake with the sense memory of holding the script in Georgie's dressing room. I felt I had discovered her in a second act of unfaithfulness almost worse than the first. That was sex, this was something deeper that bound them together. She had sworn to me that she no longer saw him, that he was absent from her life, but I could see now that this absence was filled with him, and that he would always be there between us, not just as the man who had once fucked my wife, but also as the one who had created for her something as real and vital to her existence as these beautiful boys she had created with me. It was his play, his show, his art. Everything revolved around him, including her. What she did each night she did at his bidding.

Jack and Liam, having eaten just enough to fill themselves, jumped up from the table to return to the jukebox. Fergus stayed with me. He leaned against me and said, "Dad, I'm tired, Dad."

"I know," I said. "I'm sorry. It's been a long day. We'll go to bed soon." I patted his back and cuddled him. He grew still, and it appeared that despite the noise he had fallen asleep. I moved his legs up onto the seat of the booth, positioning him comfortably, and folded up my jacket as a pillow for his head. He stirred a bit and said, "I love you, Dad," then closed his eyes.

I thought of the *I love you* Georgie had given me as we parted. She loved me, but was she mine? Was she mine, or was she gone?

"Dad," Jack yelled in my ear. "We're playing a game!"

"With those kids," Liam said, and he pointed a few tables away to a boy about their age and an older girl who was dealing from a large deck of cards. A couple of women were sitting with them, and they smiled and waved when I looked over.

"It's Top Trumps!" Jack said with excitement.

"But Dad, can we have some more chips first?" Liam asked. "I'm so hunger-y."

"You didn't finish your dinner," I said.

"But they took it away and now I'm hunger-y. I'm hunger-y, Dad."

"Okay," I said. "I'll get you some."

I walked toward the bar to order more chips and one of the women who had waved came up beside me. She was in her mid-thirties, blond with dark roots, wearing a tight black sweater. She smiled at me.

"Charming young sons you have," she said.

"Thanks," I said.

"You're American, aren't you?"

"Yes," I said.

"I'm Barbara, by the way," she said.

I held out my hand. "Peter."

"They're not mine," she said, indicating the boy and girl who were playing with Jack and Liam. "Oh no, they're my sister's."

It occurred to me she was chatting me up. Seeing no wedding ring, she must have assumed I was a single father. This was laughable under the current circumstances, and I had no idea what to say to her. That was okay, though, because she appeared to be making conversation for the both of us. I couldn't hear much of what she said over the music and the other conversations going on around us, but I nodded and smiled at judicious intervals as we fought to get to the front of the bar.

I glanced back at the boys. Jack and Liam were studiously playing cards, while a few tables back, Fergus hadn't budged. Barbara elbowed her way farther into the crowd and yelled, "Can we get some service, please?" I was growing impatient, but there was nothing to do but press forward.

Suddenly there was an opening in the crowd, and I found myself standing at the bar, a bartender just in front of me.

I turned to ask Barbara what she wanted, but when I turned back to the barman to place my order he was walking away from me.

"Excuse me," I said. "I'd like two pints of lager and an order of chips."

He ignored me. Others who had been waiting at the bar seemed to be following him as he moved across the room. Barbara said, "Hey," and caught up to him, and he finally turned and said something to her. Whatever he said made her clasp her hand over her mouth and shake her head.

"What?" I said. "What is it?"

She just continued to shake her head, but the bartender turned toward me before he strode off.

"Haven't you heard?" he yelled over his shoulder.

"Heard what?" I asked.

"The tithe barn," he said.

"What about it?"

"It's on fire."

*M*y wife's in there," I yelled to the first people I reached. Same thing I had said in the pub, to Barbara—*My wife's in there, watch my boys!*—before I took off in a dead run toward the barn.

"Georgie Connolly?" I kept calling. "I'm looking for my wife. Have you seen her? Georgie Connolly. She's in there." People looked at me with round eyes, heads shaking slowly, not knowing what to say. I wanted to scream at them—I was screaming at them, my voice hoarse and breathless already from the smoke and the running and yelling. Everything seemed to be happening so slowly. No one said a word to me, or if they did I couldn't hear them. I felt locked in one of those dreams where you're trying to say something desperately important yet no words come out of your mouth.

It wasn't until I charged forward and got too close to the fire that a fireman took notice of me. He grabbed onto me firmly and told me to get back.

"My wife's in there," I said. "My wife."

"No one's in there anymore," he said. "We got everybody out."

"Are you sure?" I asked. "Where is she?"

"We sent them all up toward the road, but you see how many have stayed too close. She'll be nearby anyway, if she was in there to begin with."

"She was in there," I said. "She was in the show." I began to look at all the people gathered around. It was the dark of night, but the fire gave off such strong light that everyone was fully illuminated. I could see each face distinctly, no shadows.

"We have got to move these people back," a second fireman told the one I was speaking to, and for the first time I noticed the heat. I was sweating, we were all sweating. Far as we were from the barn—a hundred? two hundred feet?—the heat was closing in on us.

No one seemed to care. They were all fixed on the burning barn. The open doorway, spewing flames, and the glowing lancet windows up above made the barn look like a rodent, a weasel with slitty eyes and a big snout, a monstrous, almost mythic beast attacking and in turn attacked by the men with their hoses and gear. The beating of flames sounded like the waves of a tortured ocean, the pops and cracks of whatever was burning inside affirming the absolute violence of the fire.

The barn was forty feet tall, and the flames rose almost double that height. They weren't even flames, more like one flame, a tremendous wall—very little smoke, just pure, raging fire.

Why couldn't I find her? I wouldn't believe the firemen until I saw her with my own eyes. And yet how could I find her—it was complete chaos, thirty or forty firefighters, a half-dozen fire engines and rescue vans, a crowd of a hundred at least, with more and more people arriving to watch the fire even as the men endeavored to push everyone back.

I ran toward an ambulance and spoke to a medic. "I can't find my wife," I said. "Georgie Connolly. Have you seen her?"

"We haven't had any injuries," he said. "No one was taken to hospital."

"You're sure?"

"They evacuated the building in under a minute," the medic said. "Everyone was fine."

"But what about smoke inhalation?"

He shook his head. "They all got out in time, mate. To be honest, smoke's not your problem with a fire like this. A big open space like that, there's nothing but oxygen in there. Even if you happened to be in there, it wouldn't be the smoke you'd be worrying about."

My eyes widened at this. They had made a mistake, she was still in there, no one was telling me, or no one knew. I conjured gruesome images of Georgie burning, charred—unbearable, unspeakable. I swallowed hard as nausea rolled through my body.

The guy sensed my alarm. "I'm telling you, man, your wife's fine. Our only concern here is stopping this fire. We got everybody out."

"She was in the show," I choked out. "She *was* the show."

"Oh, of course. I've seen that one walking around here. Still in her costume, she was. I recognized her because my wife dragged—took—me to the show last weekend. Not to worry, sir. She's fine, you'll find her. I would help you locate her myself, but we're meant to stay here in case we have any injured men."

He clapped a strong hand on my shoulder.

I walked away from the ambulance and continued my search, scanning faces for someone I might recognize from the crew. "My wife . . ." kept playing on my lips. I refused to believe she was all right until I could hold her in my arms.

"—can't bear to tell Piers," someone was saying, and I recognized the voice. "He's up in London. He'll be absolutely gutted." I whipped my head around and spotted Nicola in a small cluster of people.

"Georgie," I said, running up to her. "Have you seen Georgie?"

Nicola clutched my arm. "She's all right, don't worry. She was just with us a minute ago. Isn't this ghastly?"

"How can it be burning?" another woman asked. "It's all stone."

"It's the contents at first," Nicola said. "And think of it. All the posts, all the supports are wood. They're lucky there's nowhere for it to spread, really. No nearby buildings, no foliage to speak of."

"Peter."

I turned around at my name. At last it was Georgie, and I threw myself at her.

"I was so scared," I said. "I couldn't find you anywhere."

"We were so lucky," Georgie said. "That everybody got out in time, I mean. Oh, Peter, it was awful. I opened my dressing room door, and everything went up in flames. All those curtains. I don't know what happened. I don't know why no one smelled smoke." She was speaking quickly, eyes darting back and forth from the flames. "We were so lucky," she repeated.

"I thought you were—" I said. "I thought—God!" Her synthetic wig scratched my cheek, the stage makeup came off on my jacket as I held in my arms the measure of all I thought I had lost.

"I'm sorry," I said. "I'm so sorry."

Suddenly she pulled back. "Where are the boys?" she asked.

"They're still at the pub," I said. "I had someone watch them."

"I need to be with them," she said. "God, they're probably so scared."

"Yeah," I said, "I sort of took off without saying anything. I didn't want them to know."

We started across the field toward the pub, but a couple of fire-fighters stopped us almost immediately. "We have got to get you all up to the road," one of them said.

"We just want to go back to the pub," I said.

"We can't let you cross the field. The chief wants everyone back. Walk up to the road and then cross over."

"Why?" Georgie asked. "Why can't we just—"

"We know exactly how a fire like this is going to behave," the other firefighter said. "As soon as those buttresses turn from the walls, the roof will fall. It's got to, and we need everyone at a safe distance when it does. That's why we can't send anyone inside the barn, you see. None of our men. Too dangerous. We're forced to fight it from the outside. We've got forty men here, and all we can do is watch it burn. That's a hundred tons of stone roof tiles that are going to drop."

He shook his head and moved us along. Our arms wrapped around each other, we hurried up to the road. Dozens of cars lined the road, and others drove up and pulled over so that people could get out and watch the spectacle of the fire.

I felt so protective of Georgie, so connected to her, as if I myself had rescued her from the burning barn. With our backs to the barn it felt as if we were heading toward home, toward our children, each other, toward love. The heat and the tears stung my eyes and I squeezed them shut.

Just as we reached the road, we saw a small sports car driving to-ward us at a dangerous speed.

"Watch out," someone yelled. "What's that guy doing?"

People retreated to the side of the road, and then the car stopped abruptly. The driver's door opened, and a blond head rose out of the car. It was Barbara, from the pub.

"Peter," she yelled. "Your boys keep talking about their brother. They can't find him anywhere. They say his name is Fergus. Is he with you?"

*H*e had known exactly where he was going. A small boy, skating purposefully through the chaos; an about-to-turn-six-year-old who knew the secret way, the side entrance, up the steps to the dovecote, then down again into the barn; a child acting on a child's instinct, one greater than himself, to go to the last place he had seen his mother, and to save her.

Because he was so small, he went undetected until the last possible moment, when a woman in the crowd spied him and shouted, "Look, it's a kid!" It took her a minute or two to find a firefighter, a minute or two longer to convince him she wasn't just inventing figures in the flames. And then, though it was too dangerous to send men into the barn, three went in, because the woman kept yelling, "It was a child! A child! He ran into the barn!" and insisting she would go in herself to find him.

Georgie and I, up on the road, witnessed none of this, but as soon as we saw Barbara, we ran down the hill toward the barn again. If I had been panicked and desperate when I searched for Georgie, I was now beyond any such rational labels. I was feral, so was Georgie, and as the firefighters who had not been able to keep our son from entering the burning barn now prevented us from doing so, we fought them like any wild animals would. The firefighters threw me to the ground. Georgie was picked up, clutched tightly, as she screamed and clawed at her captors.

There was great cause for hope, they told us. The dovecote and stairs jutted out away from the barn—see? no flames rose from them. Our boy was probably safe; he could be in there just scared, just waiting.

The firemen had been in the barn only minutes when the roof fell. Suddenly it was quiet, darker. The fallen tiles had helped to beat down some of the flames.

It was harder to see now, and a cloud of dust enveloped the barn. We peered through the darkness, and waited.

The stairs to the dovecote remained intact and, true to prediction, so did the walls.

It could have been a minute, it could have been hours, and then two of the three men who had gone into the barn came out, coughing but upright, unhurt. Hope persisted: Fergus could be standing on the stone stairs, he could be in a place that hadn't been touched by the fire.

And then the third fireman came out, walking unsteadily, head down. In the dimmed light it was hard to see if he was staggering with injury. Several men rushed up to him but before they reached him he threw his head back and yelled, "But we got everyone out. We got everyone out." He was weeping, and in his arms he carried my son.

The men who had been holding us let go, and as we ran to Fergus, Georgie and I, to hold him and cuddle him and kiss him, Georgie let out the long scream that has never ended, that never will end, that has become, since that night, our lives.

While we waited for the firemen to find him that night, I knew I would have to tell Georgie what had happened, but afterward I waited as long as I could because I also knew it would be the last conversation we would ever have. I knew Georgie could never forgive me, and I needed her too much to let her go. I needed her as she needed me in those first days and weeks, and the only way either of us was going to live through this was to cling together, reminding each other by mere presence that our hearts still beat.

They needed one of us, I remember thinking that—Jack and Liam needed at least one of us, at least one parent. At times it seemed it would be Georgie who would make it, at other times me, but on many days I was convinced neither one of us was going to survive.

Eventually, I told her. I owed it to Fergus to tell her, because Fergus and I were the only two people in the world who knew what had happened.

Fergus and I, and now only I.

I had started the fire.

I had taken my lighter to the script of *Shakespeare's Woman* and thrown it in the little dressing room fireplace. I hadn't known it was decorative. I hadn't known that someone looking for Georgie would open the door briefly and then slam it shut, stirring enough of a breeze to blow a couple of pages across the room to ignite the curtains. Most of all, I could never have known that Fergus would awaken to the commotion in the pub and hear from strangers that the tithe barn was on fire, or that he would run straight across the field to the burning barn without bothering to search the periphery for his mother, or me, or anyone who could tell him what was happening, and instead simply slip into the barn very nearly unseen.

Who can blame Barbara for not knowing there was a third brother, asleep in the booth, half tucked away under a round wooden pub table? She never saw him. *Watch my boys*, I had told her, or maybe, *Watch my sons*. I had never told her that there were three.

Fergus knew; that is what I cannot live with. He had watched as I touched the flame to the script and he had said, "Dad, you can't start that fire, Dad," and I had said, "It's nothing, don't worry, the pages will just burn away." I simply wanted to destroy the play, the words of love from the playwright to my wife. What must Fergus have thought later when he heard that the tithe barn was burning? His mother was trapped in a fire that had been started by his father, and he would do anything to save her.

There is no accounting for a love like that. It is not a human love, invented by men and women, like the love between Georgie and me, subject to insult and cruelty, and ending. It is a godly authored love, the love Fergus had for his mother, as strong as those thick stone walls that did not fall when a hundred tons of slate collapsed onto them.

Georgie walked away from me when I told her, forever blaming me for starting the fire, just as I would forever blame her for starting what led to the fire.

I have never stopped loving her, not entirely. Each time I see her I want to wrap myself around her; every memory of our life together appears to me like an old postcard found in a book read at a country inn on some treasured weekend away. I miss her. So much, but in the way you miss your youth, or your parents after they have died. In the most final of ways, preserved with regret, no small part of yourself gone as well because the love you have shared is never coming back.

I miss her, but nowhere near as much as I yearn for my son, whose story—far more important than Georgie's or Mrs. Jordan's or my own—played out along that insubstantial strand of passion that first joined, then broke, his parents' hearts.

About the Author

Originally from Chicago, Nancy Woodruff received her MFA from Columbia University, where she won the Henfield/Transatlantic Review Award. She taught writing at Columbia and SUNY Purchase before moving to London, where she taught for eight years at Richmond, the American International University. In addition to *My Wife's Affair*, she is the author of *Someone Else's Child*. She currently teaches at New York University and lives in Brooklyn with her husband, sons, and daughter.